4/89

Arabella and the Beast

Arabella and the Beast

Rebecca Baldwin

St. Martin's Press / New York

Library of Congress Cataloging-in-Publication Data

Baldwin, Rebecca.
    Arabella and the beast / Rebecca Baldwin.
        p.   cm.
    ISBN 0-312-02163-1
    I. Title.
PS3552.A4515A89   1988
813'.54—dc19   88-12022
                                                 CIP

First Edition

10 9 8 7 6 5 4 3 2 1

For Jessica Kovar,
a writer's dream of an editor,
with thanks.

Arabella and the Beast

Chapter
One

THE HOUR WAS WELL advanced past midnight and only a few stalwart game-sters were left at the card tables of Boodles, one of London's most exclusive gaming clubs. In the card room the lights were almost out, candles near to guttering in their sockets. Two sleepy minions, no longer troubling to conceal their yawns, moved in a desultory fashion among the empty tables, placing chairs upon them and picking up glasses.

From time to time they cast longing glances in the direction of the table in the corner, where beneath the shallow glow of an oil lamp, two men, stripped to their shirtsleeves, brows covered by the green shades favoured by most experienced cardplayers, faces expressionless save for their eyes glittering with the unholy obsession of fanatical gamesters, cut the cards and drew once again.

Several piles of golden guineas lay on the green baize table between them, together with several folded slips of paper representing their vows. Yet they played on, without conversation, as if the fate of the world lay in the pasteboards they drew and discarded.

As one of the waiters shuffled toward the door of the salon bearing a tray of glasses and the remains of sandwiches half consumed hours earlier by a gamester long abed, the night porter appeared in the threshold bearing the staff of his office, a chatelaine of keys.

"Ho! Still at it, are they?" he asked in an undertone, lest the sound of human voices disturb the players.

Stifling a yawn, the waiter nodded. "It's been five hours already," he said, sighing. "My old lady's going to be proper put out with me, she is."

The night porter nodded. "And no tip from Sir Bosworth to make it worth your while, either. Clutch-fisted he is, win or lose, and it's mostly lose. Ho, I say!" he added, squinting into the darkness. "Ain't that, no, it can't be, for he's been gone to the Americas these many years now—"

"Who?" the waiter asked, with mild curiosity.

"That other gennelman, swop me if he ain't Beast Blackwater." The porter breathed, his eyes bulging with surprise. He let out a gusty breath. "Swop me," he repeated in utter surprise. "Beast Blackwater it is!"

"He's just another toff, after all," the waiter said, yawning, unimpressed and yearning for his bed.

The porter gave him a pitying look. "Well, you're new here, Charlie, you wouldn't be expected to know," he said kindly. "But you're lookin' at one o' the nabbiest gamesters there ever was! Never did we think to see him back in London, not after what happened. But then, his pa's dead,

2

so I hear, so perhaps he thought it right to come home again."

The waiter looked a little more interested as he cast a glance over his shoulder at the saturnine man discarding his hand. "What's that you say?" he asked.

The porter shifted his unlit pipe from one corner of his mouth to the other. "You wouldn't recall it, you probably bein' still in nakeens when it happened, but when the old lord was still alive, my lord Beast yonder kicked up a dreadful dust! One of the Hell and Glory Boys he was, and a Corinthian to boot! There never was such a one as he was to take any dare, accept any challenge, do anything. That's why they call him Beast, d'you see? Oh, he were a wild 'un and no mistake, until the duel. Killed 'is man he did, and had to leave the country."

"Duel?"

"Oh, my, yes. A dreadful dust there was, a lady involved, as I recall, and the long and the short of it was he quarrelled so violently with his pa, who was, mind you, as rough a man as his son, and off he went to the Americas. Never thought we'd clap eyes on him again, until I see him sitting there tonight, a-gaming with Sir Bosworth!"

The waiter looked again at the two men with interest. The one the porter had designated as Beast was younger, as dark as a Moor, with lean hawklike features and thick dark hair falling over his brow. His deep-set eyes were in shadow, but by the slight upward curve of his thin mouth it was easy for an experienced observer to tell that he was pleased with the direction in which fortune was taking him.

"He's a mean-lookin' one," the waiter observed.

"Aye, and he'd have to be to play with Sir Bosworth, don't you know," the porter returned cryptically.

By contrast, the other man, the Sir Bosworth of whom they spoke, looked as soft and shapeless as a suet pudding.

He had long ago run to fat, as much from excessive drinking as from food, and there was about him the look of slack self-indulgence belonging to a man who is no longer in control of his own pleasures. An enormous belly was barely constrained by a heavily embroidered waistcoat, and the points of his collar had long ago wilted with perspiration. In contrast to his dark opponent's face, his was bright scarlet, his expression petulant and perhaps a little frightened, as he looked down at the cards he had just picked up from the pile on the table.

"All I know is," the waiter said, shifting his heavy tray from one arm to the other, "that Sir Bosworth's been playing heavily since suppertime, and losing pretty heavily too. Few men will play with him anymore, you know, for he's neck or nothing, and it's known that he's put out his vows all over town. Up the River Tick, they say, and still he can't put the cards down. Well, around eleven this other fellow, my lord Blackwater, as you say saunters in, lookin' like a devil was in him. Weren't too many gennelmen left by then, but the ones who was still here took their leave right short after he come in, you can see why, him lookin' as if he were already foxed, and callin' for another bottle, and Sir Bosworth, well we all know he's a five-bottle man. So, with no one else, they sat down to play, and here they still are!"

"No love lost there," the porter remarked. The clock in the hallway chimed the hour of two.

"Well, sir," said the gentleman called Beast as he played his hand, spreading the cards on the table before him, "you seem to be in the lack."

Sir Bosworth threw his cards on the baize. He was sweating profusely, and his eyes stood out from their pouches.

"Damn you!" he growled, and the smell of the brandy on his breath was strong. "I say, damn you, Beast!"

Blackwater laughed. It was not a pleasant sound. He realized, dimly, that he was as drunk as his opponent, and that it was making him reckless—or worse than reckless. But he could not stop himself. "Do not curse me, sir! Rather you should curse Lady Luck, who has been singularly cool toward you this evening." One long hand reached out to scoop up the pile of guineas and notes on the table, but with an amazing swiftness, Sir Bosworth's fat fist gripped his wrist.

"One more hand, Beast! Winner takes all," he gasped.

Blackwater raised his eyebrow quizzically. "Really," he heard himself saying, the words slurred, "I do not think you should play further! I have all your vows before me, and I doubt, my dear Sir Bosworth, that you have anything else worth wagering." He had been in a foul mood when he had come into Boodles that night; his reception there among his peers, as well as the astonishing amount of liquor he had drunk, only served to make him more savage—more determined to push this sweating piglike man to his limit. He had never liked Sir Bosworth Ivers, and tonight, after several hours at the table with him, he positively loathed him.

But the gaming fever was upon the man, and even in his besotted condition Blackwater drew back slightly as Sir Bosworth leaned across the table toward him. Dissipation was engraved all over the man's countenance, in the tiny red lines that hatched his mottled face, in the mad look in his red eyes. The hand that desperately clutched Blackwater's wrist was cold and clammy.

"One more wager, Beast! One more!" Sir Bosworth hissed. "I will reclaim my losses from you. I *will*!"

"And what would you wager?" Blackwater asked. "All the world knows you're knocked to flinders, man! Your estates in entail, the bailiffs at your door! What would you wager?"

Sir Bosworth licked thick lips. His eyes narrowed, piglike in the massive flesh of his face. "All the world knows also that you only returned to London because you must marry in order to inherit your father's fortune," he panted, enjoying the way in which Blackwater winced at this truth. "Just as all the world knows that no respectable female would ever marry you."

Black rage burned in the Beast, but with effort, he remained outwardly calm as he inclined his head, removing his hand from the other man's grip in order to pour more brandy into his glass. "It is amazing what all the world knows," he said, and Beast watched the other man carefully as he shuffled the cards, his fat hands trembling.

"One of my daughters, sir. One of my useless daughters! Eating me out of house and home, no good to me! But good for you! Marry one of my daughters, and you may claim your father's fortune and satisfy the terms of his will!"

Since Sir Bosworth had spoken little more than the truth about Beast's condition, there was very little to be said upon that account. But Beast merely smiled his lazy, twisted smile. "You were always the family man, Sir Bosworth! In that respect, as in all others, you are so much like your friend the Regent!" Sarcasm hung in his tone, but Sir Bosworth was beyond insult. "Wager or not?" he asked.

The black demon that had been dancing about the edges of Beast Blackwater's mind all night suddenly struck, and took full possession of the viscount's sensibilities. He laughed wildly. "Why not?" he asked. "By God, why not?"

The hand was dealt. Sir Bosworth discarded two cards, picked up two others. An oily smile crossed his face.

His face in shadow, Beast studied the hand he had been dealt, discarded three and drew three more. Without a word, he spread them on the table. Two aces, three queens.

"Damn you," Sir Bosworth breathed, throwing down his hand. Two kings, one queen and the knave stared up at the players.

"Excuse me, gentlemen, but we must close now," the maître d' said, appearing in the shadows timidly.

"You heard the man," Beast drawled. "Time to go home, Ivers."

The other man glowered as he finished off the last of his brandy, wiping a hand across the back of his mouth. "Damn!" he muttered, rising unsteadily to his feet. "You may call upon me tomorrow to collect your prize—and much good it will do you!" he said to Beast as the waiter helped him into his coat.

Beast, shrugging off the offered assistance with his own corbeau-hued jacket, lurched a little. "Why not do it now?" he asked. He knew he had done something mad, but he was powerless to stop himself.

The demon within him was determined that this hand should be played out to the end. "Yes, why not now?" he repeated. "Collect my wager here and now! Take the lady to Gretna Green!"

"Lord Blackwater, Sir Bosworth, I must implore you both—too much to drink!" The maître d' said. In the darkness the waiters and the night porter watched this drama unfold with something akin to horror.

"Perfectly all right, my good man," the viscount said airily. "Come, Bosworth, let's have a look at these daughters of yours. One of them will be Lady Blackwater before the day is much older!"

Chapter Two

"MISS ARABELLA, MISS ARABELLA, you must get up," said the familiar voice of Butterworth, the Ivers' butler on Half Moon Street. "It's your father again."

It was an old refrain to Arabella Ivers, and, sighing, she brought herself out of a deep sleep into wakefulness with the ease of long habit. It always was, she thought, yawning and opening her eyes to see Butterworth standing by her bed in dressing gown and slippers, his old face full of woe in the light of the candle he held. She was in no way surprised to be thus wakened in the middle of the night, for a lifetime of her father's drunken caprices had inured her to indignities and emergencies.

"Has he been carried home again?" she asked, shivering as she reached for the dressing gown at the foot of her narrow bed. The room, where no fire was ever lit, was chilly on such winter evenings as this. "Is my stepmother quarrelling with him?"

"There is another gentleman with him, Miss Arabella, and I fear that they are ι.οt to be reasoned with. He sent me to fetch you, as well as Miss Lucy and Miss Harriet and Lady Ivers. Her ladyship is in a terrible pet."

"My stepsisters, too?" Arabella asked, slipping her feet into her mules. "Good God! This is something dreadful!"

Butterworth, who had been in service with the family for a number of years, pressed his lips together firmly. Of all of Sir Bosworth's daughters, he was the most fond of Miss Arabella. It had been a dark day for her when her father had married again, and to a dreadful shrew who made no secret of her preference for her own offspring, much to Arabella's grief, he thought. And now there was trouble again, and there would be a row, and Miss Arabella would once again have to smooth everything out. It went beyond what was human, he thought, to see such a good, kind soul as Miss Arabella plagued and tortured by such a family—a drunken father, a virago of a stepmother, and those two stepsisters, as spoiled and shrill as their mother.

As if she had read his thoughts, Arabella patted the ancient butler's arm. "I shall take care of it, Butterworth. But please, do you have one of the footmen stand by."

"There's only George left, Miss Arabella. Edward quit yesterday."

Arabella sighed. She could not blame servants who gave notice after a week or two of her stepmother's tongue, but it did make things difficult.

With the butler bearing the candle behind her, she went down the darkened stairs into the hall, where an amazing sight met her eyes.

Lady Ivers, her hair still in curl-papers and a highly embroidered dressing gown wrapped about her uncorseted figure, stood with a daughter on either side, tucked beneath the mantles of her trailing sleeves as she shrieked at their father, who was collapsed and sullen in the footman's chair, obviously on the verge of drunken stupor. A second man, younger, tall, thin, dark and almost satanic looking, leaned negligently against the console table, watching her with contempt in his eyes.

Lady Ivers's shrieks were almost unintelligible, but it was this stranger who caught Arabella's attention, for she had never seen anyone like him before.

She could not precisely say what made him look satanic; perhaps it was the way his dark hair curled back from his widow's peak, or the way his thick eyebrows shot up at the language her stepmother chose to use in her rage. Perhaps it was his thick black pantaloons and coat, and the black tie he had knotted carelessly about his neckcloth, but there was something in his attitude that was faintly redolent of hellfire and brimstone to her. Perhaps, she thought a little giddily, the devil had come to collect on a bargain with Papa. Certainly her father was not above wagering even with the Prince of Hell.

Some instinct for self-protection made Arabella stay where she was on the stairs, and she watched with growing unease. Clearly this was not simply another one of Papa's drunken escapades. Something worse, much worse, must have happened.

"You shan't have either of my daughters, Bosworth! I shall tell you that right now!" Lady Ivers was screaming, and Lucy and Harriet for once were deadly quiet. It was unfortunate for those two debutantes that they resembled their mother, both sadly bracket-faced, and poor Lucy having a decided tendency toward spots. In contrast to the simple merino dressing gown Arabella clutched about herself, they both sported robes of the very latest couture, for Lady Ivers always made certain that her daughters were well dressed. Arabella, at twenty-four, had long ago been consigned to spinsterhood and the position of burden upon the family, while her stepsisters, having been out for two Seasons, had received a great deal of push from Lady Ivers to establish themselves credibly. Unfortunately neither of them had taken, but, as Lady Ivers explained, it was important that they be presented in the very latest modes. What she did not say was that she hoped their singular lack of looks and charm would be compensated for by a great many ruffles and ribbons. Unhappily, this scheme had not done its magic.

Sir Bosworth, who disliked all of his daughters equally, frequently complained about the bills their debuts had brought him, but Lady Ivers plunged ahead heedlessly, and of a consequence the family was deeply in debt. Even Arabella knew that, and she hoped that her father had not lost a great deal to this gentleman.

"A wager is a wager," Sir Bosworth was saying, his massive head falling toward his waistcoat as consciousness slipped away. "Pick and have done, Beast!"

"Not my daughters!" Lady Ivers was screaming. "I'd kill you before I'd let you touch one hair upon my girls' heads!"

To Arabella's amusement, it appeared as if this dark gentleman were somewhat repulsed by the two packages of curl-papers and cucumber lotion defended by their mama.

"A wager is wager. And I promised him a daughter to wife, and a daughter he shall have," Sir Bosworth slurred.

The other gentleman nodded. He, too, Arabella perceived, was drunk, terribly drunk. Instead of being horrified, she was amused. So, now Papa had wagered his daughters' hands? How very silly of him. It couldn't possibly be legal, could it, she wondered. Or moral. Or something. She pitied the man who would offer to marry either Lucy or Harriet. Clearly, this was too much.

Before Lady Ivers could start up again, Arabella came down the stairs and into the light. "Pray, what is this?" she asked calmly, turning to the dark gentleman as the only person who seemed coherent enough to answer her question.

"It is very simple," he said with vast dignity, returning her slight smile with one of his own, as if they were two persons of sensibility and sense who had found themselves caught up in an unpleasant scene not of their making. "Your father wagered me tonight at Boodles for the hand of one of his daughters—that is, I presume Sir Bosworth is your father?" He looked as if he could not quite believe there was any kinship between this calm, auburn-haired woman in a plain merino dressing gown and the rest of her family, who were beginning to remind him very strongly of one of Cruikshank's crueler prints. Oh, he knew how drunk he was, and he knew he was utterly mad, but the demon was upon him, and Beast meant to carry this through to the end. He had never backed down yet, and he was not about to start now. He only wished that this stupid woman would stop shrieking, and that her two stupid daugthers would stop crying, and that Sir Bosworth would stop attempting to pass out in the footman's chair.

"I am Arabella Ivers," she said clearly. "This Lady is my stepmother, and these are my stepsisters. Am I to understand that my father has lost one of us in a card game?"

"Faro," the dark gentleman said, nodding mournfully. "Blackwater, at your service, ma'am." He lurched a little. "Er, I don't suppose you could get Lady Ivers to stop screaming?" he asked.

"Papa wagered us in a card game?" Arabella repeated. She felt a sense of repulsion, not just toward her father—

12

for whom she had long since ceased to hold more than filial duty—but at her stepmother's vulgarity, and her stepsisters' stupidity. The two had now begun to snuffle and not so very softly, either.

Blackwater nodded.

"Well, you can take her and give me the notes he gave you, curse him!" Lady Ivers exclaimed. "She's all of a piece with him, anyway." In the shock of the moment, Lady Ivers had lost all pretense to the gentility so assiduously cultivated over the years since she had married a baronet. "You can have Arabella!" she shrieked.

Twenty years of her stepmother's abuse and neglect were settled in one moment of Arabella Ivers's life. If Beast Blackwater's demon was dancing in his head that night, some forgotten spark of the gambler's instinct Arabella had inherited from her father was ignited. In that surreal moment, she saw her past stretching into her future. The thousand set-downs, the cheeseparing little indignities, the endlessly drab and distasteful life spent with a drunken wastrel of a father and an encroaching mushroom of a stepmother. A thousand petty tyrannies and slurs were recalled and an existence singularly lacking in any sort of joy until now were reviewed in a second.

She looked at Blackwater and could not entirely dislike what she saw. Whatever he offered her, it must be better than this, she thought, and in a second, her decision was made.

"You wish to offer marriage, sir?" she asked.

"I do indeed," he replied, bowing slightly.

"Than I will consent to marry you."

A thin thread of sobriety flashed in his eyes. Fear, horror, self-loathing, apology. But Arabella, having made a decision to take charge of her own future for the first time in her life, was not to back down. "I think," she said in a voice that quavered only slightly, "that if I were to spend one more night in this house, I would go mad. Would you be good enough to wait for me while I dress and pack a few things into a bandbox? I will not be long."

Her bravado touched his, and he inclined his head in assent.

"Miss Arabella—" Butterworth protested as she ran up the stairs past him, but it was already too late.

In a quarter hour she was down again, dressed simply in a drab pelisse and an untrimmed felt bonnet. In her hand she carried a bandbox, and her chin was high as she walked down the steps to meet her husband.

"You leave this house young lady, and you don't come back, do you hear? You're a bad, wicked girl to be going off like this, and with Beast Blackwater, too!" Lady Ivers shrieked, her wind evidently having shifted. "Who's going to take care of your sisters if you leave, hey? I'll have to get a lady's maid, and your papa won't like that!"

"Bella's really leaving?" whined Harriet, wide-eyed.

"It's not fair!" Lucy cried. "Bella gets to be a viscountess and we're not even married yet!"

"Be quiet, do!" Lady Ivers shrieked, slapping Lucy very hard, an unprecedented gesture when directed toward one of her own daughters. "You come back here! You come back!" she shrieked at Arabella, who took the arm Lord Blackwater offered her as he led her somewhat unsteadily toward the door. "You come back right now! You wicked, depraved girl! What will your father say?"

As Lord Blackwater opened the door, and Arabella stepped out into the snow and the early dawn, she turned briefly and looked back.

"He will say," she answered quietly, "that I have discharged his debt, as an Ivers should." She squared her shoulders and looked up at Beast Blackwater.

"Do we go to Gretna Green?" she asked naively.

Beast looked down at her. Suddenly he began to laugh. "By God, yes! Yes, Gretna Green by all means!"

Chapter
Three

THE DEMON OF THE previous night was now having its revenge, for when Beast awakened, his head felt as if a thousand tiny, infernal creatures were all at work inside his skull at once, digging out his brain with picks and pitchforks. With some effort he managed to crack open his eyes slightly, perceiving the unmistakable sunlight of a late autumn afternoon, and found it so painful that he immediately squeezed his lids together again. An attempt to move his aching body was met with the strongest resistance from his protesting muscles, and he allowed a single, regretful groan to escape his parched lips.

"I think," said a genteel female voice somewhere near, "that if you were to drink just a little of this, you would soon feel very much more the thing."

Beast felt something wet and cool touch his lips, and he opened his mouth and drank. Whatever it was it tasted inutterably foul, and he sat up in bed, coughing and hacking. It was some moments before he could force himself to open his eyes, but when he did, he clutched the bedsheet to his chest and stared. "Who—" he gasped, horrified.

Arabella Ivers, in a bottle-green gown twice turned and carefully darned, a carefully pressed ribbon wound through her auburn curls, met his gaze with cool and steady green eyes. She shook her head. "I think you would feel better if you lay down and didn't try to think for a while," she said matter-of-factly. "I have had some experience with the blue devils, you see. Papa is much accustomed to them—"

"Who are you?" Beast demanded, unheeding of her advice. "What are you doing here?" To be certain where *here* was, he glanced quickly about himself, and was in no way reassured to see that he was lying in the great Chinese bed in his own room at Blackwater House on Grosvenor Square.

"You brought me here last night," Arabella said. In her lap there was an embroidery frame; as she spoke, her needle, threaded with pink yarn, darted in and out of the linen, forming a pattern of roses in long and short stitches that were only slightly unsteady. "I am Sir Bosworth Ivers's daughter. You won me at cards at Boodles, I believe."

Beast collapsed against his pillows with a groan. Unfortunately, due to years of neglect, they were filled with dust, and he began to cough again. Arabella handed him a handkerchief, which he waved away with a limp hand, and a goblet of her unspeakable blue-devil remedy, which, lacking any other liquid, he was forced to drink.

"This is awful stuff!" he gagged. "What is in it?"

"Nothing you would want to hear about right now, I

think," Arabella replied in a matter-of-fact voice, as if she found herself in the bedchambers of strange men every afternoon. "But I promise you, in a minute or so, you will feel very much more the thing."

"If I'm not poisoned first," Beast muttered. He pressed a hand against his throbbing temple, and noted with interest that he was still in his shirt of the night before. "How did I get here?" he asked. "Did you undress—"

Two faint spots of colour appeared in Arabella's cheeks. "Oh, no! Your man—he seems to be the only servant you have—" Finally nonplussed, she lapsed into silence, the needle betraying her emotions as it darted in and out of the cloth in her lap.

Beast found himself watching this movement with a sickened fascination, as if he were suffering from mal de mer, and closed his eyes again. "Miss Ivers!" he said, sighing. "Good God! I hope I—you—oh, good Lord!" It was not an entirely irreverent cry, wrung from the lips of an anguished man who has only just begun to recognise the extent of his previous night's folly. "That woman! Those girls! Shrieking!" he exclaimed, shuddering with the memory. "Miss Ivers, what have I done to you?"

A piece of yarn was snipped with a tiny pair of scissors; another selected from the workbag in her lap. Arabella placed her concentration into threading it through her needle.

"Nothing, Lord Blackwater. You were going to take me to Gretna Green, but I decided that it was out of the question to try to journey to Scotland when you only had five pounds in your pocket. I have not travelled a great deal, but I think a journey all the way to the border would cost a great deal more. Post chaises and inns and postilions and so forth," she added absently, and thought carefully.

"I collected it would be better if we came to Blackwater House."

"Gretna Green." Beast repeated. "Miss Ivers, what can I say? There is no apology I could make to you—your honour! Your family!"

Although she was but four-and-twenty, the eyes that looked at him were old and weary. "My honour is my business, and as to my family, I can assure you that they are very glad to see the last of me, as I am them. It was not a happy situation, as you might have guessed from last night's scene. Believe me, Lord Blackwater, I would have done anything—*anything at all*—to escape! Another night under that roof and I think I should have gone mad—or run away on my own!"

Beast contemplated this for a moment as his mind began to clear of its cobwebs. He turned his own actions over in his mind, and cursed himself for his usual impetuousness. Once again it had landed him in trouble. "Punishment for my sins!" he muttered aloud. But he had begun to feel better. His head had stopped pounding and his mouth no longer felt stuffed with cotton wool. Bit by ugly bit, the events of the previous night began to unravel in his mind's eye with a singularly unappealing clarity, and he lay among his dusty pillows and wondered, not for the first time, how in thirty years of living he always seemed to find a way to get into every predicament that offered itself.

"I took the liberty of telling your man, Fishbank, is it? Yes, that you would wish a light breakfast. A poached egg, tea, toast and butter. There is nothing so disagreeable as a fried egg when one is blue deviled, you know."

"I know," Beast said with a sigh. He cast a look at the woman who sat on a chair beside his bed. She was not, he noted with some disappointment, a great beauty, but then, recalling her stepsisters, he shuddered yet again, and thanked fate for that small mercy. Although his tastes had always run to opulent blondes with a worldly air about them, he had to admit that she was more than simply passable, with good clear skin and green eyes fringed with long lashes. She had a short nose and a small budlike mouth set into a wistful expression in a heart-shaped face. Her auburn hair was thick and curly, at the moment bound up in a ribbon with braids wrapped about her ears. Two tiny dimples set at either corner of her mouth led him to believe that she was not unused to smiling, and he reflected that he had not given her a great deal to smile about. At least, he noted, she was not looking at him with repulsion, and that, he supposed, was more than he had any right to expect at this point.

"Tell me, Isabella—" he began.

"Arabella," she corrected him gently, driving the needle through the linen and drawing it out again, leaving a line of blood red behind it in the rose petals.

"Arabella, then." Had he really stolen away a woman named Arabella? "Why did you come away with me? Surely you must have known my reputation—"

She frowned, concentrating on her stitching, refusing to meet his eye. "I told you, my lord, that anything was preferable to staying where I was. You saw where I lived, you saw my father and my stepmother and my stepsisters. Whatever you have to offer me, it cannot be any worse than that. And if you have sobered and changed your mind, I suppose I might prevail upon you to lend me some money so that I could put up somewhere while I seek employment as a governess in some respectable household? Only, I suppose, now I am not quite so respectable! I must become used to that, I suppose, but I imagine there are a great many disrespectable households where a governess would not be unwelcome. Perhaps some of the royal *bâtardes* or some such thing—"

Beast heard himself laughing. It was not an accustomed sensation, and at first he had some trouble recognising this sound as laughter, and the laughter as coming from him, at that. It exhausted him and he lay back again, closing his eyes. "There can be no question of that! I may be a dreadful man, but I am no despoiler of well-bred young ladies! For you and I there is but one course, Miss Ivers. We must be married today!"

"Well, I was rather hoping to hear you say that," Arabella replied. "It would make everything so much easier, you see. I am really not qualified to be a governess. My French is dreadful, I have no Italian at all, and I wouldn't know how to use the globes if my life depended upon it."

Beast laughed again. It felt good. "At least you have a sense of humour," he said, noting the smile that danced in her eyes as she spoke. "That is good. It has been a long time since anyone has made me laugh."

"A most improper and deplorable sense of humour, I fear," Arabella replied. "At least my stepmother always reassured me that it was so! But I am very glad that you want to marry me. It certainly would solve both our problems, since you informed me last night that you must needs marry to claim that part of your inheritance that is unentailed, and I must needs marry to escape my family. Shall we deal together a little?"

"We must! For I see no other choice in the matter, Miss Ivers. I have dishonoured you by bringing you to my house, you know, to stay the night without so much as a housekeeper to guard your respectability. Not," he added darkly, "that I am any great advocate of marriage! My last marital encounter was—" He broke off, frowning. "But let us not speak of that! I am certain that you are as knowledgeable of that old scandal as I! It would seem that all of London is! We will not speak of it."

But Arabella was ignorant of any details of Beast's

reputation, much less his history, and wondered, just for a second, if she would have done better to have stayed on Half Moon Street. In a second, her common sense restored her faith. Certainly, she thought, there was nothing disagreeable or sinister about Blackwater this morning. Indeed, he looked only faintly satanic propped up on his pillows in his shirtsleeves, and that probably had as much to do with the thick shadow on his jaw as with the way in which his eyebrows grew and his hair descended into a widow's peak. In fact, she felt, for a man with a decided case of the blue devils, he was being remarkably civil, all things considered, and that was a good sign.

"I suppose you will have me, Miss Ivers?" he asked, rather formally, under the circumstances. "That is, be honoured and all of that if you would be Lady Blackwater. Try not to get in your way or make you unhappy. Can't promise—know m'self too well for all of that, but try to make you comfortable anyway, and not stand in your way."

If, in the years before she had been consigned to the shelf, Arabella had dreamed of a marriage proposal, it would not have come from a man in the throes of wine sickness, nor would it have been a string of hastily and abruptly uttered phrases. Clearly Lord Blackwater was a man uncomfortable with the proprieties, and uneasy with convention. Flowery phrases and grand gestures were totally alien to his character. But Arabella had made her decision the previous night. She would have followed the very devil himself into the hottest reaches of hell, she would have shipped herself off to Botany Bay in a sea chest, before she would return to that other hell, that other penal colony on Half Moon Street.

"I would be pleased to accept your offer, my lord," she said evenly. "Thank you for asking me."

"Mind," said Beast uneasily, "it need be a marriage of convenience only! Eventually, of course, we shall need to produce an heir, but we need not think of that right now, or indeed at any time in the near future," he added, pressing his hands to his aching head. "Mean to say, I'm not the sort who forces himself on a reluctant female, and all of that."

Arabella tilted her head to one side. Her manners were happily not missish. "No, I quite understand," she answered him sensibly. "The circumstances are rather—difficult."

"Well," Beast said, sighing in great relief, "I'm glad we understand one another on that point. Not the sort of man who beats m'wives, either, or kicks up a dust about the bills, you'll find."

"I hope I shall be—equally complaisant," Arabella said softly. She could not resist adding, with an imperfectly straight face, "And I promise *you* that I shan't beat my husband, either!"

Beast made a sound that might have been a laugh, and waved at her dismissively. "That's a good girl. Now go you and have Fishbank make you some breakfast, then put on your wedding finery. And tell him, as soon as he's finished, to attend on me. I shall, much against my better judgement, have to remove myself from this bed and get dressed if we must needs procure a special licence and all of that mummery. We cannot respectably pass another night under the same roof unless we're buckled." With a great effort, Beast sat up and held his throbbing head in his hands. "Let this be a moral lesson to you! Four bottles, yes, six bottles perhaps! But five bottles—*never*! Oh, Lord, I shall never do that again!"

Chapter
Four

HAPPILY, BISHOP BLACKWATER WAS among the handful of his numerous relations Viscount Blackwater had avoided estranging in his long career, and not even the full truth of this brief engagement, presented over sherry in his study, seemed to rattle the worldly and sophisticated Blackwater, prelate of a large and fashionable bishopric. Reminiscenses of boyhood pranks were laid out in his study, along with the necessary papers, and he gravely wished Arabella the best of bridal luck in her new endeavour as Lady Blackwater.

For Arabella, it seemed as if the brief, almost casual ceremony were a dream from which she would awaken at any moment. With the sexton and the janitoress as witnesses, one thin dark man joined her in matrimony to another, right there in his study, faintly redolent of ancient mildew and dry rot, of all old churches. Above Cousin Paul's head, a Raphael of the Virgin and Child stared down at the curious scene, as impassive a witness as the young and muscular sexton and the prim, janitoress, who still held her apron in her hands when she made her mark in the register book. Arabella, a dun-colored merino pelisse covering her old bottle-green dress, a dowdy bonnet covering her auburn curls, heard herself saying "I will" when Paul asked her if she would take this man, Philip Aubrey Charles Christian, to wed. She heard her husband's names for the first time and thought them strange, such an odd string of names. She heard the viscount say "I will" in his deep, rumbling voice when the bishop asked if he would take Arabella Mary Catherine Ivers to be his wife. Suddenly there was a plain gold band on her finger; where it had come from she did not know, save that as he placed it there, her husband—her *husband*, good God, what had she done?—whispered to her, "You shall have something better from Rundel and Bridge very soon."

She had but a minute to stare at the ring gleaming dully on her finger before it was all over. Then, more to please the witnesses than anyone else, the viscount's lips touched her cheek. It was a chaste, dry kiss, and Arabella knew she was a wife, *his* wife, married to a stranger.

"Allow me to be the first to congratulate you, Lady Blackwater—Cousin Arabella, if you don't mind!" The bishop smiled, holding out his hand.

Arabella felt as if she must have stared at it stupidly for hours before taking it into her own and smiling, murmuring something she hoped was appropriate.

The bishop offered another glass of sherry and was refused by the viscount. Arabella signed her maiden name for the last time in the parish register. I am now Lady Blackwood, she thought with wonder, and with the bishop's promise to call with his wife upon the newlywed couple in due course, they left the church and returned to Grosvenor Square in a hackney carriage.

"I suppose I shall have to have a look-in at Tattersall's now," Beast muttered absently. "Daresay we shall need something to drive. All I've got is my hacks for the park."

"Yes, I suppose so," Arabella replied, looking at the front of the hackney without really hearing what he said.

Within two hours they were back behind the doors of Blackwater House, this time as man and wife.

The viscount, with all the air of a man who has awakened early to perform some necessary but inconvenient errand, tossed his high-crowned black beaver on the empty footman's chair and yawned behind his hand. "If you do not mind," he said, "I would like nothing better than to return to my bed. My cursed head continues to pound, and I think it best if I lay absolutely still for a few hours."

"Just as you like," Arabella replied, still in a daze. She watched in dismay as a cloud of dust rose from the red velvet on the footman's chair.

"So good," Beast murmured as he headed wearily up the stairs, holding his aching head in his hands.

Arabella now had her first good look at Blackwood House. Last night it had been dark, and this morning she had been far too concerned with the turbulent events of her own life to give much more than a passing glance at her surroundings. But now, left to her own devices, she was experiencing a profound sense of dismay.

She could see from where she stood, slowly undoing the strings of her bonnet, that what was not draped in Holland covers was covered with a thick, white layer of dust and cobwebs. While accustomed to the slatternly household of her stepmother, Arabella found this much, much worse. She drew off her York tan glove to run a finger over the surface of a gesso table, leaving behind a wide streak of dull golden surface.

It seemed to her a great shame that such a large and magnificent house should be so carelessly maintained that she could find no clean surface upon which to rest her pelisse and bonnet.

Like most of the grand houses along Grosvenor Square, Blackwood House was Palladian in design, with the grand salons opening off the hall on the ground floor. Built as a town residence for some long-deceased Blackwood, it had been, no doubt, a grand place fifty years ago, but now curtains were rotting on their rods, upholstery was shredding to dust, and the rugs beneath her feet were sadly threadbare from years of footsteps over their pale Aubusson surfaces. It was impossible to distinguish what lay beneath the thick blackness of a gold-framed painting beneath the staircase, or what had once laid in a glass case by the blackened fireplace. Cobwebs hung in festoons from the chandelier, bagged in a linen cover, and Arabella was almost certain that roaches, rats, and worse ran behind the elegantly carved wainscoting.

Gingerly she picked up the skirts of her green merino and tiptoed across the floor into what was, she supposed, a grand salon.

Gilt furniture had been dulled by years of dirt—neat layers of grime embedded the ornate French carving of some forgotten cabinetmaker. A large set of Stuart candlesticks on a side table were so blackened with tarnish as to be the color of ebony. Large strips of the brocade wallpaper had peeled away from the wall, and hung forlornly over a set of Louis XVI chairs. "Rising damp," Arabella clucked to herself. It seemed a very great waste to neglect such lovely things, particularly when she recalled the parade of cherished objects that had moved in a steady procession out of Half Moon Street, headed for the pawnbrokers and the dealers, while the little cash that returned went to support Sir Bosworth's gambling and Lady Ivers's wild extravagances.

As she moved through the large, silent rooms filled with ghostly shapes of furniture draped in holland covers, dust and cobwebs stirred from years of slumber, moving sullenly in the thick dark air. Here there was a green room filled with japanned furniture and the sort of huge ornamental Delft pieces that had been popular a hundred years earlier. Arabella touched a flower pagoda nearly as tall as she, marvelling at the griffins, sphinxes and moors twisting about its shape. She wondered how many years it had been since someone had placed flowers in it; cobwebs festooned it now. The next room was carved with Grinling Gibbons's touch, the paneling ornamented with baskets of flowers and fruit and garlands of wooden vines and roses, and sadly laquered a very black colour, perhaps to match the Jacobean furniture, all black walnut and covered with a particularly nasty shade of bilious green, shot with tarnished gold thread. She had reached the end of the house, and when she turned back she noted, without any particular pleasure, a pair of marble heads, obviously the product of some previous viscount's Italian tour, staring coldly down at her from the portal above the door.

In the opposite wing she found the painting room, filled with a great deal of Chinese Chippendale, highly carved in just such a way as to afford the most resting places for dust and upholstered in swagged and fringed brocade of what must have been at some point a rather garish shade of ochre, now faded to a watery yellow. She would have drawn back the curtains to allow in the sunlight, save that the ancient draperies seemed to be rotting away; at her touch, an area as large as her hand simply disintegrated into yet more dust. So she had to content herself with peering at the darkened paintings very closely, squinting and standing on tiptoe, her nose within inches of the huge canvases as she attempted to discern their subjects. Here again, Blackwater House seemed to have been under the influence of the Italianate; most of the works were, as best she could tell, given their ancient and grimy condition, of the Italian masters of the late Renaissance. A great many of them tended to depict, in a very unhappy fashion, the various atrocious martyrdoms of some very obscure saints. Thinking of her new husband growing up among such sights made her feel a little sad; these were hardly the subjects to cheer a child, or even an adult, and after the most cursory inspection, she passed into the next salon.

Here she found the monumental proportions and heavy gilt work that styled William Kent's pieces, together with several pier glasses, the mercury sadly chipped, as well as an enormous Grinling Gibbons fireplace and what appeared to be a number of family portraits. Certainly all the characters depicted in their quaint and heavy clothing bore a striking resemblance to her husband, being to a man (or a woman) long of feature, dark of cast and decidedly sinister in appearance, with the widow's peak very much in evidence everywhere.

Generation after generation of them stared down at her through dark, imperious eyes, as if they were judging her and finding her decidedly unworthy to join their lineage. Here were the Blackwaters, hundreds of years of them, all heaped together and doubtless full of a very untidy set of histories, dragged about by the present scion and his heirs like a ball and chain. It was an uncomfortable sensation, to feel that one was being watched by whatever ghosts inhabited that vast and silent house where not so much as a clock ticked on a mantlepiece. Arabella shivered slightly, wishing her shawl were not flights and flights of stairs away.

Beyond this salon there was the ballroom, a vast and empty space with ornate baroque moldings on the walls and a set of Linnel ballroom chairs scattered about, making it look even more deserted and empty. It was separated from the salons by a set of French doors, and after trying the handle in the shape of a bear's paw and finding it unlocked, Arabella slid through and stood, reluctant to progress any further, shivering in the cold. There was not much to recommend the room; in the stillness she disturbed, crystals in heavy chandeliers sighed and tinkled beneath their covers like the revenant of some lost music from a forgotten evening. She took a step back and felt her hair brush something. Turning, she nearly gasped, for it seemed that a human hand protruded from the molded wall, holding the empty sconce of a candlestick. With revulsion she noted that this image repeated itself a hundred times about the room, each hand holding an elaborate Corinthian sconce. That all the hands had been painted in flesh tones made it somehow all the more horrific, and she was glad that she was not modeled upon the heroines of the Gothic novels then in vogue, or she might have fainted dead away; those hands simply looked a little *too* lifelike for her tastes. She backed out of the room and was glad to close the doors behind her, even if it meant facing down the satanic ancestors once again.

She was fumbling with the latch when she heard someone cough behind her. She started, a hand against her breast as she spun around.

"Oh," she said, a trifle irritably, "It's only *you*."

Fishbank, his lordship's man, instantly looked apologetic. "I am so sorry, Lady Blackwater. I did not mean to startle you. Although if you will allow me to say so, it is a house that startles people."

It was hard to imagine Fishbank startling anyone. A few years younger than Lord Blackwater, he was as cherubic in appearance as his master was demonic. Nothing could have been less threatening than his round and rosy countenance, generally set in a jovial expression, topped by a very full head of blond curls. Having been in the service of Beast Blackwater since that gentleman had been at Oxford, Fishbank was completely unflappable under any circumstance, and absolutely devoted to his employer's interests. His behaviour of the previous evening, when a lesser man would have given notice, had immediately endeared him to Arabella, who was grateful for any sign of kindness in a fellow human being.

"I put his lordship to bed, and he seems to be sleeping quite peacefully," Fishbank informed her. "I think by tonight you will see him much more the thing, my lady, if you will permit me to say so. But I only came to offer my congratulations to your ladyship and to offer to be of whatever assistance you may need."

"And I think I shall need a great deal," Arabella said frankly, returning his smile. It said much for Fishbank's presence of mind that he seemed in no way curious or even disturbed at the circumstances by which his master had arrived at matrimony. Perhaps he had been with Beast Blackwater far too long to wonder at anything that gentleman might decide to do. "Thank you, Fishbank. It seems strange to be called Lady Blackwater. I daresay I shall become used to it in time, but right now—" she made a small gesture with her hands, and Fishbank inclined his head.

"Just as you wish, my lady," he replied. "I thought you might wish to see the house. I should apologize for its condition. The late lord preferred the country in his last years, and when we returned from America, all was as you see it now. The caretaker, well, my lady, he was an old pensioner of the late lord's, and as you can see . . ."

Arabella nodded, looking about herself. "How long has this place been shut up?" she asked.

Fishbank screwed up his face in memory. "I would guess over a decade. My lord departed for America six years ago, and four years before that, well, the first Lady Blackwater, that is to say, his lordship's first wife, Miss Barbara, only used to stop here for a week or two at a time in the Season."

Arabella felt a queer sensation in the pit of her stomach. "His lordship's first wife?" she asked blankly.

For once, Fishbank looked slightly dismayed, but he recovered himself. "Yes, my lady. Miss Barbara. It was an unhappy thing, surely you recall?"

Arabella shook her head. "Six years ago, I was just barely out, you see."

Fishbank sighed, as if he were making a decision. "If you will permit me, ma'am, perhaps it is best if I enlighten you, since it is not a topic that his lordship enjoys discussing. It was six years ago—no seven—when the duel took place, you see."

"The duel," Arabella repeated. Somewhere dimly, she recalled hearing that Lord Blackwater's exile had concerned a duel. But since they moved in entirely different circles, she was abysmally ignorant of her husband's history. Dear Lord, she thought, what I have I gotten myself into? Whatever it is, she reminded herself sternly, it is better than Half Moon Street, think of that. "Please, Fishbank," she said aloud, "I think it best if you tell me what happened."

Fishbank nodded. "Yes, my lady, I think it best if you hear it from me, who has his lordship's interests at heart, rather than someone who—well, his lordship has his enemies, m'lady. His ways are abrupt and sometimes rude, and take getting used to. But Miss Barbara, well that is she, over there in the corner, that painting done up by Mr. Lawrence, not long after she married his lordship."

A few paces brought them to a corner of the room, where Fishbank pointed upward at a round portrait of a young lady.

"She was beautiful," Arabella said simply, studying the smiling, dark-haired woman with a hint of arrogance in her pale blue eyes, a sensuous attitude conveyed in the way in which she turned her body toward the viewer, and in the alluring smile, confident that men wanted her.

"Oh, yes, my lady, Miss Barbara was quite beautiful. And very spirited, too. There's those that say that Sir Thomas Lawrence didn't do her justice in that portrait, but he caught the attitude toward her, if you take my meaning."

"I think I understand," Arabella said, uncertain why she should feel her new life threatened by a dead woman. After all, this mad contract had nothing at all to do with love. But here was the sort of woman her new husband had loved. Or had he? She wished she could ask Fishbank, but she knew the lines that lay between servants and masters, no matter how close they might seem.

"Well, my lord and Miss Barbara knew each other from childhood, you see. There was never another lady for my master, and it was Miss Barbara or nothing. The old lord was dead set against it—he never did like Miss Barbara, not from the start, nor her family neither, you see. If you'll pardon me, my lady, it was as if the old lord knew that two people as strong willed and headstrong as my lord and Miss Barbara would fall fatch soon enough. But my lord's as hardheaded as all his family ever was." Fishbank gestured about the room, at the portraits scowling haughtily down at them from the dingy walls, as if disapproving of this interloper and this manservant daring to discuss one of themselves. "And in the end, he married her. They quarrelled almost from the wedding day, ma'am, for both of them were intent upon having their own ways, and even though I was raised up on the estate, and my father butler to the old lord for thirty-five years and more, rest both their souls, I would tremble to hear them quarrelling and arguing, afraid one of them would kill the other, there was that much temper between them. But they were both young, and their friends were a fast crowd, if you'll forgive me, my lady, too much drinking, too much gaming, too much—well of everything, and both of them you know, seizing life with both hands, bein' so young and handsome a pair. But his lordship's got a temper, ma'am, and when that Polish count started droppin' rumours there and the other place that his relationship with Miss Barbara was more than just friendly, if you'll pardon my meaning, well, my lord's a gentleman, and whatever he thought about Miss Barbara by then, or she about him, she was his wife, and he *had* to call his man out."

"The duel," Arabella said softly.

Fishbank looked extremely uncomfortable at the turn his narrative was taking. It took a little effort on his part to continue. "You will, of course, hear rumours my lady," he said, his usually sanguine face full of earnestness. "Lord Blackwater called out the Polish count; what other choice did he have when Miss Barbara's—ah, friend, was slandering her name all over London?"

"Any gentleman would have done the same, I suppose," Arabella agreed, thankful that this was at least one scandal her father had managed to avoid dragging the family through.

"They will say that he killed his man, but he did not. Although I believe he could have, had he wished. I believe, my lady, that he deliberately deflected—the count was wounded in the shoulder. My lord never misses his target, my lady. But of course it was a dreadful thing. That very night, Miss Barbara and her Polish count departed for Italy, where I assume, they are more inclined to be indulgent about such liaisons than the English. One need only look at Lord Byron . . ." He coughed discreetly. "However, I digress. While Miss Barbara and her count fled the scandal to Italy, my lord had a terrible falling out with his father. Harsh words were exchanged, unforgivable things were said between father and son, and my master departed for the Americas, vowing never to return until his father stuck his spoon in the wall, as he phrased it. I fear the old lord was right, that Miss Barbara created a great deal of trouble, just as he had predicted she would, and brought a great deal of scandal down upon the family name. The old lord was a high stickler, ma'am; a gentleman who believed in respectability. Well, Miss Barbara caught the Italian fever in Italy and died within a year, and is buried there. And we wandered about the Americas, hunting and fishing and looking at all the wonders of the old *ruinas* in Central America, but that's another story, and happier one, our adventures in the Americas." He nodded.

"Pray continue. I must know, Fishbank, and I have a feeling that you will tell me all, without embellishment, so that I can understand."

He licked his lips. "Well, the old lord died, as we thought he would, proud to the end, and too stubborn to admit to any reconciliation between himself and his son. But so determined was he to prove his point that he left a codicil in his will that we never knew of until my lord returned home to see what you find here."

"And that was?"

"Well, my lady, as you must know, my lord's estates and properties are ruled by entail and mortmain, and there was naught the old lord could do to prevent my master from assuming the title and the entailed properties, of course. But the bulk of the old lord's fortune was his own, do you see, and he could leave it just as he liked. Oh, the lord was a good man, my lady, don't mistake me. But he would have the last word, even if he had to reach out from beyond the grave to do so. So, he set things up with his man of law that my master could only inherit if he could find a respectable female of good breeding willing to marry him. An Englishwoman, d'you see, and a lady of respectability. I disremember how it all read, in that legal cant solicitors are so happy to use and the rest of us can't make head nor tail out of it, but that was the catch. Now, here's my lord, proud as fire, with a terrible scandal hanging over his head, and an estate that cries for the money that comes from the income of the old lord's private fortune, and what set of parents are going to allow their daughter to marry a man with so evil and dark a repute as Beast Blackwater? Them of course not knowing my master as I do, you see. I doubt even the most heartless parent would offer a daughter to such a man as my master has been painted to be in his absence from this country. And a mushroom—a merchant's daughter or one of the American nabobs' daughters, that wouldn't do, of course. The old lord was very clear on that point; she had to be a lady of the utmost respectability and a good family. So, you see, you came into our lives when we needed you the most."

"I see," Arabella said thoughtfully. "It all begins to make sense to me now." Again, she wondered what a single act of impulsiveness in an otherwise dull and ordinary life had gotten her into, and again she reminded herself that whatever lay before her could be absolutely no worse than what she had left on Half Moon Street. Or could it?

But her father had been a crony of the Regent's for far too long for any sort of on dit to shock her sensibilities, and she shook herself briskly out of her reverie.

"I thank you for telling me these things, Fishbank," she said gravely. "I hope you will feel no regret in taking me into your confidence. The circumstances are so unusual—"

"Oh, my lady, my master and I have dealt with matters under much more unusual circumstances than this in the past few years. Why, when we were captured by the Keche Indians—but I think that such tales are better left to my master to tell. I only hope, my lady, that I may serve you as I serve my master, and I await any commands you might have." The smile returned to his face and he looked at her hopefully, as if expecting her to pull order from this vast chaos of a house.

"To begin with, I am very hungry," she said. "I have only had toast and tea for breakfast, and I do not know what we shall have for dinner tonight, but I imagine a nourishing meal will make his lordship feel very much more the thing."

Fishbank turned his palms outward. "Bachelor's fare, ma'am," he said, sighing. "In general, when his lordship and I are at home, I send around to Claridge's for a meal. I might reassure you that you will find few occasions when you need deal with his lordship's blue devils. In the Americas, we became more moderate in our intake of spirits, and have, in general, accustomed ourselves to more temperate habits.

"In the old days, his lordship was a five-bottle man," Fishbank continued, "but nowadays, it's only when he's in one of his brown studies, and most times then, he just retreats into himself, if you know what I mean, my lady. In the old days, they all drank a great deal of blue ruin, the ladies too."

In the long afternoon that stretched before her, Arabella had ample time to brood over these statements. From somewhere, Fishbank produced a luncheon of cold beef, cheese and apples, and finding her in the library, went over the menu for dinner with her. Apparently there was no end to the man's talents, for he suggested dishes Arabella thought would have been far removed from his ken, such as veau d'angoulème and sole meunière with one or two removes and asparagus, which he seemed confident he could produce even so far out of season.

After this conference, he disappeared upon his own mysterious errands, and Arabella was left to her own devices. If it occurred to her that this was an extremely odd way to spend one's wedding day, she consoled herself with the knowledge that she would have her wedding dinner with her husband, and she was glad. It was within her nature to desire to please him in whatever way she could, and she was curious as to the man she had so hastily married.

"Marry at leisure, repent in haste," she said aloud to the book-lined walls, cutting a piece of apple. She had not realised how very hungry she was, and she ate with gusto, studying the room in which she found herself.

Here, at least, a cheerful fire was piled high with wonderful scoops and scoops of extravagant coal, and in the scuttle on the hearthstone, there was yet more. Fires were a rare thing on Half Moon Street, usually lit only in Sir Bosworth's and Lady Ivers's bedchambers and in whatever room they happened to be spending time. To escape from the family was to escape from warmth in winter, and Arabella had endured many a freezing hour in her bedchamber, huddled beneath counterpanes and quilts simply for the pleasure of solitude and relief from tears and storms belowstairs.

To find herself in a room lined with books, ensconced in a soft and comfortable chair before a bright fire, was Arabella's idea of purest bliss. She propped her feet up on the fender in a most unladylike gesture, surveying her environment. Unlike the reception and staterooms on the ground floor, the rooms on the first story were smaller and more intimate, designed for the comfort of the family and its friends, not for the ostentatious display of Blackwater wealth. Here again there was Grinling Gibbons paneling, but it was softer and more mellowed than the stately arrangements below, created to enhance shelf after shelf of wonderful books, and full of country themes such as birds in flight, flowers in bloom and sheaves of wheat bound with chaff stalks. One or two paintings hung on the walls, good sturdy landscapes, doubtless studies of Blackwater country houses rendered with academic precision rather than with passion.

On the table beside her were piled a number of current periodicals, she noted, including the daily newspapers and such reading material as the *Turf Gazette* and the *Gentleman's Repository*, together with one or two penny boardsheets of George Cruikshank's nastier caricatures. Idly she picked one up and felt a small, electric shock pass through her as she immediately recognised the face of her husband savagely picked up by the pen of the satirist, from his bushy brows to his widow's peak. He was seated in a chair with a woman in his lap; opposite them, on the other side of a table filled with empty wine bottles and the remains of a huge dinner, an elderly man, crowned with a pair of deer's horns, snored, oblivious to Beast Blackwater and the woman he was caressing. Arabella fancied herself reasonably sophisticated, but she had trouble understanding why the snoring old man should be crowned with antlers. Easy enough for her to understand why the woman was sitting in Beast's lap, however, spilling her bosoms out of a tight dress and wearing a great necklace of diamonds that she fingered with beringed hands while she leaned toward Beast. Even Cruikshank could not make her ugly, with her masses of blond hair and her huge eyes, hand-tinted blue.

"Lord and Lady S—— Entertain at Home," the caption read, "or, a Beast for Dinner."

Enlightenment dawned upon Arabella instantly, and she was surprised and discomfited to find that she was feeling a sharp pain of jealousy toward this Lady S——, whoever she might be. Arabella had been an habitué of Half Moon Street far too long not to know that men kept mistresses just as ladies took lovers, and that one looked the other way, but still, she could not help but wonder about Beast Blackwater and this pretty Lady S——. Not, she reminded herself firmly, that she had the least right to feel anything. The marriage that had taken place this afternoon had been a business arrangement and nothing more. Blackwater had indicated to her that she was in no way obligated to him, nor he to her. And yet, as she studied the sharp, cruel lines of Cruikshank's evil genius, she felt a sense of dismay, a faint pricking at her new security that left her slightly empty.

"Gossip!" she said aloud, and balled the broadsheet up in her hand, throwing it into the fire. Unfortunately it missed the licking tongues of flame and landed behind the fender, where it lay in the darkness of the shadow.

Arabella rose from the chair and shook herself, as if to cast off this shade of ill feeling that had crossed her mind. The curtains had been pulled across the windows, and she released them, together with clouds of dust, in order to allow the last of the grey London daylight to filter into the room. On the opposite side of the Square, she noted that someone would be having a party tonight; the wagon from Gunter's, the caterer's, was pulled up before the house, and the footmen were rolling out the carpet and lighting the torches.

She turned away, shaking out her thin wool shawl about her shoulders, and browsed among the books.

The Blackwater who had journeyed to Italy had evidently been the last great reader in the line, for most of the volumes she encountered at first had to do with the antique and classical studies of that country's history. He had commissioned beautiful bindings for his collection, she noted, and ran her hand along the dusty spines of leather-bound works of Suetonious and Josephus, regretting the dusty smell of mildew on them as much as her own disinclination to delve into their writings at this moment.

She admired the polychrome decorations of a German Bible's jacket and the embossed and raised gold chasing of a Bestiary, illuminated in gilt and polychrome by some monks long dead. She paused over a work on botany, admiring the lovely prints; she paged through a homely copy of *Culpepper's Herbal*, evidently well used by generations of Blackwater ladies, for it was stuffed with receipts and clippings concerning such domestic esoterica as removal of red wine stains from silk, a lotion of beeswax and cucumber to improve the complexion, and a certain remedy to kill the moth in furs.

But she could not have been happier had she discovered a treasure when she apprehended that her late mother-in-law had been an avid reader of the novels of the Minerva Press.

Novels had been on the Index at Half Moon Street, Lady Ivers believing firmly that fiction corrupted and sensualised the minds of young ladies, causing hysterics and romantical notions that must be ruthlessly suppressed. With this in mind, Arabella piled yet more scoops of coal on the fire, settled back into the soft and comfortable chair, propped her slippers on the fender, reached for an apple and proceeded to browse happily through such masterworks of fiction as *Horrida; or, The Vampyre's Revenge, The Haunted Monk of Weyburn Abbey* and *Castle Grue*, all by Miss Webb, her very favorite authoress, quite lost to time and place, and as happy as if she had finally found a safe haven after years of torment.

For several hours, Arabella skimmed through the adventures of very silly maidens, very heroic, if somewhat pompous heros, gloriously melodramatic villains and highly improbable supernatural situations.

It was the first time in her twenty-four years that she had been able to relax in a room by herself, deliciously warm, surrounded by books and other homely objects without fear of interruption or invective on her sloth and laziness from her stepmother and stepsisters, and she revelled in it so completely that it was with a start that she looked up to see that the room had grown quite dark, and the clock on the mantel advised her that she had only a little time to dress for dinner.

With a guilty start, she reluctantly closed the second volume of *Horrida* and scurried to her room.

Her portmanteau had been placed in the rose chamber that connected to Blackwater's rooms, and she was surprised, when she opened the door, to find that her few shabby gowns were in the wardrobe and that a bright fire burned in the carved marble fireplace beside the gilt and rose damask–hung bed. As if by invisible hands, a jug of hot water and linen towels had been laid out for her in her little dressing room, together with her horn comb and brush and the little silver hair receiver, all that she possessed that had belonged to her late mother.

In such grandeur, all rose and gilt, Arabella's few possessions looked dowdy and insignificant, but it was with hopeful hands that she took down her one good gown, once turned and twice made over since her debutante days. It had once been celestial blue silk, but time and wear had faded it to a pale grey shade, and in spite of the band of lace she had added to the neck and hem, it still remained a somewhat forlorn and faded air, like a shabby genteel countess who has seen better days.

Nonetheless, it was the best dress Arabella had, and she carefully put it on, turning this way and that to look at herself in the spotted pier glass, marvelling at the luxury of having such a mirror all to oneself. What she saw did not compare to favourably, in her eyes, with the Lady S—— of Cruikshank's print; her hair was auburn, a most unfashionable shade in an era that prized blondes, and, while thick, had a deplorable tendency to curl and wave, at a time when the craze was for thick, straight tresses. She was of medium height, with ample bosom and hip, and alas, the epitome of beauty was tall and candle-thin. She tended, no matter what, to freckle, in an epoch where alabaster white skin was the only possible shade for a lady's complexion, and her nose was decidedly retroussé, when style demanded one's proboscis resemble that of a Roman statue. She had clear green eyes, but her lashes were almost colourless, and her stepmother had frequently informed her that she resembled her mother's family, the Beauforts, far too much to have the least pretension to anything other than *jolie laide*. Indeed, she had heard herself characterised so often as plain that she quite believed herself ugly, and had long ago given up any attempt to utilise what she had to her best advantage, as a more confident female might have done. However, tonight, she took special pains with her hair, braiding it up about her head and curling the errant tendrils about her finger, and pinched her cheeks to flood them with colour before fastening about her neck a string of seed pearls, the only inheritance she had managed to preserve from her late mother, and indeed, her only piece of jewellery.

She had a spangled gauze shawl, cast off by Lady Ivers, and this she draped about her shoulders. She winced as she pulled on her gloves, hoping that the darn would not show too clearly by candlelight.

With a deep breath, Arabella turned and left the room.

The hallway was lit by low-burning lamps. She had not noted that, like the sconces in the ballroom, they were supported by human hands, and she shuddered with distaste as she gathered her spangled shawl, inadequate in the chilly passage, about her shoulders and descended the stairs past a singularly unattractive painting illustrating the fate of Acteon.

Only one doorway stood open on the first story, and it was toward that faint light that she made her way in the dingy twilight of the hall, past a series of sporting paintings depicting the kill in various attitudes.

Peering into the room, she perceived that it was the *salle à manger*. Lit by a sideboard loaded with Carolingian silver candlesticks, a vast table gleamed faintly, seeming even more enormous for its lack of all covers save one, at the very end of the room. Fronted by perhaps twenty Jacobean chairs, with an enormous, empty and very tarnished silver epergne placed squarely in the center of the board, the dining room table seemed to go on forever.

Anxiously, Arabella peered into the gloom for some sign of her husband. All that met her eye were the dim and hulking shapes of various oversized pieces of Carolingian

43

and Jacobean dining-room furniture, hard and grotesque shapes caught in the dim light of the fire burning on the hearth and the gutter of the candles.

"Ah, I find you here, my lady," Fishbank said, bustling into the room with an apron tied about his livery. "If you will be good enough to allow me to seat you, I shall pour you a glass of wine before dinner is served."

"But where is his lordship?" Arabella asked. "I see only one place set."

Fishbank's smile flickered slightly on his cherubic face. It was clear that he disliked being the bearer of bad news, for he coughed discreetly. "His lordship sends his regrets, ma'am, but he prefers to have his dinner in his room tonight. I fear," he added in his natural voice, "that his lordship still feels the effect of the wine, ma'am. Brandy will do that to him. Brandy and Holland gin, it's all the same, and his lordship *will* go and drink them, anyway."

Deftly, Fishbank guided Arabella to the head of the table, where a single cover had been set. The Georgian silver was badly in need of polishing, but the china was finest Meissen, done in the zoological motifs popular in the time of Beast's grandmothers. Arabella noted with some interest that her dinner plate was painted with the likeness of a wolf, while her server displayed a pheasant.

A glass was placed to the right of her plate. In the gloom, Fishbank's hand seemed disembodied as he poured a splash of blood-red wine into the crystal goblet.

"I thought we might dispense with the sherry tonight, since I managed to find this excellent Merlot in the very back of the cellar. It is a '98, and probably laid down by the old lord himself, for he was quite particular about his wines." Fishbank hovered over her shoulder, the bottle at the ready as Arabella sipped. It was excellent—fruity and full—and she nodded.

"Very good," she managed to say, as the manservant filled her glass.

"Light, yet fruity. I fear that we shall see no more of that particular vineyard for some time to come, as it has been sadly ravaged by the late war. Perhaps in a year or two—but who knows?" Fishbank mused, placing on the table a tureen featuring a porcelain porcupine. Before her he placed a soup dish with a fighting cock, and proceeded to ladle a delicious-smelling liquid into it.

"Just a soupçon of garlic juice makes all the difference with a stewing mutton," he said, stepping back to allow Arabella to sip at the broth. It was delicious, and she looked at Fishbank with respect.

"You are a man of many talents," she offered. "Wherever did you learn to cook? For you must have cooked this—it could never have come from a hotel kitchen."

Fishbank bowed his head in acknowledgement. "A man's man, my lady, learns to do a little of everything, like Figaro. But I am pleased that you like it." He bowed his way out of the room, and in a while returned with the sole, so light and succulent that it seemed to melt in her mouth with the first bite. Then he brought in the veal, with a remove of haricots and ratatouille. With each of these he changed the wine—a fumé blanc with the fish, a delicate burgundy with the veal, all the while acting as footman as he stood behind Arabella's chair and served her from the sideboard.

For dessert he produced a champagne and a charlotte bombée, but Arabella, after one bite, sighed and shook her head.

"Too full! Too full!" she almost cried. "Fishbank, if you always cook like this, I shall be as big as the Rotund Lady at Astley's!"

Fishbank smiled at the compliment, removing the

plate. "I am very glad you like it, ma'am," he said. "Since there are no gentlemen to table tonight, I shall leave you with coffee. If you need me for anything, you have to but to ring."

Arabella thanked him, watching as he made his way down the length of the long dining room and disappeared out the door.

The bottle of champagne stood in its silver bucket at her elbow. She eyed it, and then her glass, half full, and poured out a cup of coffee.

When the door closed behind Fishbank, the room seemed to be filled with a terrible tomblike silence. The only sound was the flame licking at the coals on the hearth. Not so much as a clock ticked, and when she stirred sugar into her coffee the sound of the spoon against the side of the cup was as loud as a scream.

Arabella looked about herself, at the huge dark shapes of the furniture, the long, endless length of the table, the shadowed arches above her head, the disapproving paintings on the wall full of grim landscaping and gloomy people (it was too dark for her to perceive what they were occupied in doing), and felt as if she were no bigger than an ant before a doll's house.

An overwhelming feeling of loneliness overcame her; for a moment, and a moment only, she wished herself back on Half Moon Street where, at this time of night, a servant would loudly be giving notice, Lady Ivers would be shrieking remonstrances, and Sir Bosworth, preparing to leave for the evening's revels, would be roaring at his valet over a missing shirt stud or tie-piece. Lucy would be playing the pianoforte, badly, while Harriet sang, equally badly, their cacophony floating upward through the house from the depths of the ice-cold drawing room.

Somewhere within this massive, dusty tomb, her

husband did whatever husbands did, and his manservant washed the dishes and perhaps thought about slipping down to the local for a pint with his friends.

And Arabella sat like a captive within the chilly, formal dining room, a single, insignificant human being, drinking a single cup of coffee at a table designed to hold upward of twenty.

A carriage rolled down the street outside the long windows, the prosaic sound of horses' hooves and rolling wheels jolting the self-pity out of her.

With a sad little giggle that echoed in the hollow room, she rose from the vast table and fled to the more supernatural if no less haunted, ambience of Miss Webb's novels.

Chapter
Five

THE TIERCE, PEALED FROM the bells of St. Margaret's church, awakened him, and Beast Blackwater, feeling human again, threw back the covers and climbed out of bed, pulling the bell cord to summon Fishbank.

All circumstances considered, his mood upon this morning was far better than a man in his circumstances had any right to expect, and there was only the faintest twinge of guilt for the way in which he had treated his new bride on the previous day. Such feelings were alien, in general, to Beast; he pleased himself, and cared very little for the good opinion of anyone else. However, a vestige of conscience reminded him that *some* attention was due his wife, and he peered into the mirror above his shaving table as he warily made his ablutions.

Not a vain man, he had always considered himself perfectly suited to the name Beast, for he gazed at his own reflection and perceived a very ugly man indeed, whose dissipations must certainly be engraved into the lines on his face. He leaned forward and peered into his own eyes, searching for telltate red in the white, and, finding none, felt slightly reassured.

A trifle impatiently, he rang again for Fishbank; it was unlike the man not to respond, with coffee and toast, to the first call of his master.

Anxious to present himself in as favourable a light as possible to his new bride, Beast wasted no time in lathering his jaw and scraping the razor over his own face. Although he was perfectly capable of shaving and dressing himself, he felt a twinge of resentment that on a day when it was important for him to look as presentable as possible, Fishbank was not here to assist him in his levee. After he had dragged the razor over his stubble, Beast pulled the cord once again.

Unlike some of his more dandified friends, he needed no assistance in pulling on either his smallclothes or his trousers, for they were not so tight as to require that he be sewn into them every morning. But as he buttoned his waistcoat and arranged his cravat, his mood began to turn a trifle surly, and he jerked violently at the bell pull this time. Really, he needed Fishbank to arrange the folds and style of his neckcloth just so! Ordinarily careless of such things, it seemed to Beast to be a very great injustice that on the morning when he must needs appear at his very best, the loyal Fishbank was nowhere to be found.

After running his brushes through his dark hair, Beast was thoroughly put out, and he grasped his dressing gown from the back of the chair, threw it over his shirtsleeves and proceeded to storm down to the nether reaches of the house, all the while muttering the darkest sort of curses beneath his breath.

Although he had not been in the servants' hall since he was a boy, he could still find it easily enough, and his temper was no way assuaged when he discovered it to be empty.

"Fishbank!" he called, and his voice echoed in the stillness. "Damn the man!"

He was just about to storm upstairs again when he heard the sond of a key in the lock, and turned to watch as the delivery-entrance door opened to admit not only Fishbank, but Arabella, both of them laughing and carrying market baskets piled high with food.

As they saw him the laughter died from both their faces, and Beast was suddenly aware he must appear a perfect ogre in a very bad melodrama, looming over them in his embroidered dressing gown. But he was powerless to stop his bad temper.

"So!" he said in lowering accents. "I ring and ring and ring, and I find not only my manservant but my wife—the female I have made *Lady Blackwater*, gone!"

Fishbank opened his mouth and closed it again. Long ago he had learned to ride out these sudden squalls, which blew their course and were gone as soon as they had come, but he cast an uneasy look at Lady Blackwater.

"We have been to market," she said calmly, hefting her laden basket on the table between them, where the head of a fat pullet flopped over the side. "I did not expect to see you this morning so early. We hoped to have your breakfast ready and served you when you awakened, husband." Her tones were calm; years of dealing with Sir Bosworth's foul tantrums had inured her to such unpleasantness. "Now, if you will but wait for a second or two, your coffee will be ready and I will coddle you an egg."

"I don't *like* coddled eggs!" Blackwater exclaimed, but some of the wind was already out of his sails, and he began to look a trifle sheepish.

Fishbank had laid down his market basket and was tying on his apron. Wisely, he sensed this conversation was better left to her ladyship, and surrendered the field to her.

"I hardly expected to find you marketing, as if you were the cook," Blackwater said sullenly, but he sat down at the table nonetheless. Arabella removed her dowdy little bonnet and pelisse and laid them on a chair, revealing a dun-coloured round gown that had seen many years of use, over which she tied a kitchen apron as she removed eggs, cheese, and bread from her basket and laid them in the larder.

Arabella smiled, without looking at him. "Not only can I shop, but I can dress a joint, make pastry, and put up preserves. When servants come and go as fast as they do at my father's, it is a good thing to have some idea of how to hold household, husband."

"Husband," he said under his breath, rather liking the domestic sound of it. Aloud he said, his thick eyebrows drawing together. "Well, it will not do, you know, for a viscountess to be seen haggling over the price of eggs! That is Fishbank's job!"

"Fishbank has too much to do already," Arabella replied, laying a place before her husband. "And besides, he has been so long out of the country that he doesn't know the price of things. Only fancy, the fishmonger wanted three and six for an eel no bigger than my arm!"

Blackwater, who had no more idea of the price of eel than the other man in the moon, stared, openmouthed. His last wife, as far as he knew, had not even been precisely certain where the kitchens were in this house. The thick eyebrows rose slightly.

"Fishbank!" he cried. "Know you no better than to allow Lady Blackwater to go jaunting about town with you?"

"I insisted," Arabella said, breaking off the heel of a loaf of bread and buttering it generously before popping it into her husband's open mouth. "That will not only take the edge off your hunger, it will make your hair curl, or so my old nurse used to tell me. What would you have me do, husband? I can only sit so long in the library, as delightful a room as it is, and read. Only fancy, I quite got through *Horrida* last night, and this morning started *The Haunted Abbey*—"

If there was rebuke in this statement, Blackwater did not hear it, although he sensed his own guilt. Before he could reply, a cup of coffee was placed before him, creamed and sugared to his liking, and he sipped at it, feeling instantly very much more sanguine. "I wonder that you did not have nightmares from reading such trash," he grumped, but not quite so hard as he might have.

"Well, from now on, I shall try to read something more improving," Arabella assured him. "If you don't want a coddled egg, how about an omelette?"

"Fine," he said, and she wisely let him alone while he drank his coffee.

"I had to shave myself this morning," he said to Fishbank, sighing, when an omelette, thick with cheese and ham, was set before him. "I had to tie my own cravat."

"And a very fine job you did of it, my lord," Fishbank replied. "Couldn't have done it better myself. The style is the rone d'amour, if I am not mistaken."

After Beast had partaken of a hearty breakfast, he pushed himself back from the table and looked about. "Wife, I think we need to hire some more servants. Fishbank cannot be expected to do everything himself, now that I am married again, and I will not have my wife haggling with fishmongers. Fishbank, slip around to the registry and tell them we need to interview some people. Whatever my lady wants. Ma'am, we are not poor—in fact our fortunes, thanks to you, are on the rise! I would imagine that you might like one of those French gals to do your hair and press your ribbons?"

Arabella smiled. "I think we need an army of cleaners more than anything else. This is a lovely house, husband, but it needs to be set to rights before I can think of anything else. If you would allow Fishbank to supervise that, I think you will find it will make all the difference in your comfort."

"Just as you like," he said, although he could not imagine a female who would pass over an abigail in favor of a clean house.

"I believe I can make the necessary arrangements for that," Fishbank said. "And ma'am, I have a cousin, a fine, respectable young girl, living in Richmond, who is anxious for a place. If you will permit me, my lady, I think she would suit you much better than some strange French-woman."

Arabella smiled at him gratefully. "Yes, I think you might be right," she said. "Husband, I don't think I could contrive to deal very well with a *very* fashionable abigail!"

Beast cast a look at her dun round dress and nodded. "Yes, yes, I see," he said. "Well, would you care to ride with me in the park this morning?"

"My lady has no habit," Fishbank put in discreetly, and Arabella flushed.

Beast frowned, seeing for the first time the dowdy bonnet and pelisse lying on the chair beside him. "I see," he said, rising from the table. "Well, ma'am, that is easily rectified! No wife of mine will go around town in that quiz of a hat, I can tell you that! Fishbank, before you leave, fetch me my coat and hat and call us a hackney! My lady and I are going shopping!"

"But you just told me that you didn't *want* me to shop!" Arabella exclaimed.

"Not for food! For clothing, yes!" Beast exclaimed. He looked long and hard at his wife, appraising her colouring and figure, and then burst out laughing. "To think!" he roared, "That I should find a wife who must be asked to shop for clothes! I never thought I would see the day!" He stood up and extended his hands to Arabella, bringing her to her feet. "Come with me, wife! It is time that Lady Blackwater met the world!"

Chapter
Six

MADAM CELESTE, THE MODISTE who had held sway over the world of haute couture for two decades, had seen many things in her career, so many that she considered herself perfectly impervious to surprise. When a little vendeuse nervously appeared in her office, announcing that Lord Blackwater desired speech with her, and added somewhat breathlessly that he was accompanied by a young person, Madam merely raised her eyebrows. Only a week ago he had accompanied Lady Sibley, who was choosing a gown for her next ball.

Majestically unhurried, she finished tallying a column of accounts before sailing into the salon, hands clasped at her waist, cool smile on her face, to greet the man who had just paid five hundred pounds for a gown for his established mistress.

However, behind her smile, she wavered in puzzlement when she saw the young woman who accompanied him. Not only did she seem perfectly respectable, she was also hideously dowdy, in a perfect atrocity of a bonnet and a pelisse that appeared to have seen its heyday a decade earlier; even then it would have caused Madam to wince. But her vascillation took only a second.

"My *dear* Lord Blackwater," she said smoothly, extending her hand to the viscount.

"Good day, Madam Celeste," he drawled, relying totally upon her discretion, which was acute, "Lady Blackwater, this is Madam Celeste, who will clothe you. Madam, my wife."

It took all of Madam's formidable self-control to prevent her eyebrows from shooting up toward her hairline. Her only betrayal of emotion was the way in which she fingered the pearls at her bodice. Lord Blackwater, in her experience, was a gentleman who preferred his ladies wordly, sophisticated and vivacious. The lady who rose to her feet, smiling nervously at her, was none of these things; indeed, she had auburn hair, a shade Madam always found most challenging to attire. Even as she smiled and exchanged pleasantries with the new Lady Blackwater (*alors!*), her nimble mind was scanning the possibilities. Since Blackwater had, to her knowledge, no need to dangle after a fortune, and this lady was obviously not possessed of one, she drew a complete blank there. It came to her that this must be some sort of love match, and as rare as such things were among her clients, she was enough of a Frenchwoman to feel a slight warmth toward the girl at the idea of Beauty taming the Beast.

Well, at least there was the *potential* for beauty there, she thought, snapping into her professional genius at once. One did not have to be Lord Blackwater to see that there was a certain luminous quality behind those green eyes, waiting to be brought out by the skilled hand of such a one as herself. Happily, Lady Blackwater would not be such a challenge as some of the females presented to her, but merely a matter of exercising her particular talents to best advantage. It would cost Lord Blackwater a great deal, of course, but then he could afford it. And the girl looked so hopeful.

Madam smiled a genuine smile.

"Everything. She needs everything," Lord Blackwater was saying.

Madam Celeste's smile grew even broader. "Leave it to *me*, my lord," she said, leading the new Lady Blackwater away.

Beast settled comfortably back in an armchair and smiled at one of the pretty little vendeuses who just happened to hear his name and ventured into the showroom.

His desultory conversation was interrupted within a quarter hour, when his wife emerged from the changing rooms in a slate-blue riding habit, finished up the front with braiding and fitted at the shoulder and sleeve with military braidwork.

Beast lifted his quizzing glass to his eye and surveyed her with approval. "An excellent choice, wife," he said. "It makes you look quite dashing."

Arabella leaned over him, her face full of distress. "Husband, I fear we cannot afford this! Madam tells me it costs *two hundred pounds*!" She looked at him, wide-eyed, and Beast gave one of his rare laughs.

"A bargain, I assure you!" he replied. "As long as you like it."

"Oh, yes, I do, very much, but *two hundred pounds*!"

Beast could not conceal his amusement. Barbara and

Lady Sibley both would have thought it cheap at that price. "We'll have that," he said to Madam Celeste, who nodded.

"Come, my lady," she said firmly, "I have one or two other things that I think may suit you very well."

With a backward glance for reassurance, Arabella let herself be led away.

"*Everything* new!" Blackwater repeated firmly. "Day through night."

In a very short time, Arabella found herself in possession of such fashionable costumes as a jaconet muslin morning dress trimed with pink ribbon banding, a kerseymere pelisse in Pomona green, two walking dresses, one celestial blue trimmed with Gros de Naples runchings, the other grey Circassian cloth trimmed with white lute-string edged with cord. She had a dinner dress in sea-green Gros de Naples with a net overskirt of gold mesh, and not one but two evening dresses, one of sherry-colored Italian crêpe festooned with double runches, the other geranium twilled sarsenet valenced in blond Urling's lace.

To all of this and more, Viscount Blackwater nodded his approval, although he frowned severely at the sight of a tartan afternoon dress and an orchid carriage dress trimmed with bands of ermine. A lady, he knew, must perforce change her clothes three or four times a day in town, each time to meet the occasion, and he had no intention of allowing any wife of his to be caught without the latest and most fashionable attire. Like many men who have developed an appreciation of women, he had an eye for what displayed a female to her best advantage, and his taste was impeccable, if instinctual. Not for him the posturing of a dandy who would know the difference between a pellerine and a ruff; he simply knew what he liked, and said so.

As Arabella was being assisted into a cottage dress of

dun bombasine trimmed in peach satin by no less a person than Madam herself, one of the vendeuses appeared in the curtained doorway of the trying room, bearing over one arm a richly trimmed ball gown of silk barege. "Pardon me, Madam," she said, "But is this laid aside for my lady? It has Lord Blackwater's account on the tag."

"Oh," Arabella said, sighing, before Madam Celeste could protest. She reached out and fingered the material, in awe. "It is beautiful. How could he know?"

"I fear there has been some mistake," Madam Celeste said with a dark look at her assistant. "This gown has been promised to Lady Sib—to another lady."

"But there cannot be," Arabella said, her bargaining instincts aroused. "My husband's name, as the vendeuse has pointed out, is on the account tag. Oh, it is lovely. His taste is so good—" She began to slip out of the cottage dress. "I must try it on at once," she said breathlessly. "My husband will be so pleased."

Madam sighed, with a look at the vendeuse. What could she possibly do, she wondered. A week ago, Blackwater had chosen this very gown for Lady Sibley, his current interest, and now his wife wished to try it on. She rolled her eyes heavenward, seeking assistance from whatever deities look after the fortunes of modistes. Alas, there was no intervention from that direction, for Arabella had taken the ball gown and was slipping it over her head, turning this way and that to look at herself in the pier glasses that lined the trying room.

"It *is* lovely," she said with a sigh.

And indeed it was. If Madam was hoping to protest that the jonquil-colored barege was the wrong color, or that the rich, foamy material made my lady look fat, or that its tiny bows on sleeve and corsage were unbecoming, or that its banded and rolleaued hem made her look a dowd, she was disappointed.

Surveying Arabella with a cold and dispassionate eye, she was forced to admit that it was far more flattering to this auburn-haired lady than to its original model, the blond and pink Lady Sibley. Even so, she twisted at her pearls and pursed up her lips, feeling obligated to utter more protest.

"My lady, I am very sorry, a stupid mistake with the tags, this dress is promised to another lady. It has already been spoken for."

"Surely," Arabella replied with the mulish look she took on when she knew she wanted something, "there must be some mistake—you see? Right here, on this clip, there is my husband's name." She fingered the slip of paper attached to the ceinture.

"A mistake, I am certain! Alas, my lady, I fear that it will not do."

Madam Celeste was capable of overbearing even the most imperious of her clients, and her will was certainly equal to that of Arabella, who reluctantly removed the gown and pressed it back into the relieved arms of the open-mouthed vendeuse.

"The blue-and-white crepe and sarsenet," Madam said firmly in a tone that promised a dressing-down later, and the vendeuse scurried away.

"Now, this cottage dress, ma'am, I can see that it would suit you very well," Madam said smoothly, feeling very much as if she had averted a major disaster right there in her showrooms.

In the end Arabella came away with a ball dress of fine white tulle trimmed in ethereal blue, over a white satin slip richly trimmed in Brussels lace and crêpe lisse. It was very pretty indeed, but her heart remained with the jonquil silk, and she sighed at the memory of it.

When Lord and Lady Blackwater left Madam Celeste's, Arabella was wearing a roan pelisse trimmed in silk bands of braided gold, a look of mixed astonishment and satisfaction upon her face. "I am so very grateful," she exclaimed to her husband as soon as they had entered the hackney. "No one, not even when I made my debut, has ever bought me such wonderful clothes!"

Blackwater, happily ignorant of the close call the ladies in his life had had behind the scenes, was of a mood to be pleased by his new wife. No woman had ever been grateful to him before simply for doing his job as a man and providing her with clothing suitable to her rank in life, and he found the experience novel.

"The next stop will be the milliner's, for I will not have you walking about with that dreadful thing on your head, and then I will direct you home, for I am to Tattersall's, where of course no lady must go. But I hope you will trust me to select a hack for you? You must ride with me in the park, you know."

"Riding, yes," Arabella replied, sighing. "I have felt the lack of a horse more than anything else." No daughter of that notable neck-or-nothing Sir Bosworth Ivers could be anything but an equestrienne; it had been his only teaching to his offspring. She proceeded to charge her husband with a great many things that she sought in her ideal horse, and he promised to see to them all. "I have always thought it quite unfair that ladies are not permitted in Tat's," she finished. "Perhaps they think we shall outsay the men!"

She was, however, somewhat mollified by their expedition to the milliners' shops in Bond Street; she came away with a riding hat of cork covered in grey bombasine and set with a very dashing plume over one ear, to go with her slate-blue habit, a *toque à la russie* of jade *peluche*, a gypsy hat ornamented with Austrian feathers, an ivory bonnet of *velours simulé* with a full *ruche* of celestial blue, a pinceau velvet bonnet lined with white satin with a wreath of roses, and a morning cap of Bristish net with knots of pink ribbon.

"Now, as to gloves and shoes and all the other fripperies that women seem to be unable to live without, I'll leave that to you," Blackwater said, as he took his leave of her at the end of Bond Street. "Only understand this; no nip-cheesing and no worrying about the cost! I want always to see my wife turned out in the very best style, as befits a Lady Blackwater, and tell 'em to send the bills to my man of business!"

Arabella smiled. "Just as you wish, husband!" she exclaimed, and in very good book with him, she directed the hackney back to Upper Mount Street, feeling as if she were the most fortunate woman on the face of the earth.

She arrived at home to find that Blackwater House had been invaded by an army of busy workers. Windows had been thrown open to expose the sunlight to the dark and dusty rooms; mops, brushes, and ladders were everywhere in sight.

In the midst of all the hubbub stood Fishbank, wrapped in an apron and busily directing his minions as they cleaned and polished and dusted and washed the house from top to bottom.

"All the brasses must be removed and boiled in very hot water, then wiped instantly," he was saying. "That will keep them from tarnishing, you see." He looked up and saw Lady Blackwater. "Good afternoon, ma'am, as you can see we are all at sixes and sevens, but I hope that within a very few days, we shall have the whole house cleaned and sparkling. Your packages have been arriving in steady stream all afternoon. I have placed them in your dressing room, where my cousin Eliza Stackpole is unpacking them. I hope you will find her satisfactory, ma'am, she was an undermaid to her aunt, the great Stackpole, Lady Stockwood's dresser. However, I fear you shall have to wait a bit for the interview, for Mrs. Blackwater-Younge has arrived, and I placed her in the library. I tried to persuade her that she might find you at home tomorrow to company, but she would not be deterred." Fishbank smiled, took a deep breath and bowed.

"Mrs. Blackwater-Younge? In the library?" Arabella asked, all at sea.

"Your sister-in-law, my lady," Fishbank whispered. "My lord's only sister."

"Good Lord! And the house in such a roar, and me in my hat and pelisse and this old dress!" Arabella exclaimed.

"Mrs. Blackwater-Younge has been waiting for over an hour, my lady. If you would like to go directly up to her, I will bring along Madeira and cake shortly."

"Thank you, Fishbank. Please tell your cousin I shall be with her directly."

With the feeling that she was not unlike Anne Boleyn on her way to the headsman, Arabella climbed the stairs and crossed the long hallway toward the library, wishing with every step that her husband were here to support her in this ordeal. If his sister was anything like Beast, then she had a great deal to dread, Arabella thought, particularly since her marriage must, of a necessity, come as a shock to his only sister.

She closed her eyes and placed her hand on the brass knob before turning it, taking a deep breath.

It only took one glance for her to see that Mrs. Blackwater-Younge fulfilled all her expectations. To begin with, she had the look of her brother about her, the same long, thin face and dark complexion, the same widow's peak. She wore a dreadfully fashionable black-and-white bonnet ornamented with a great many ostrich plumes. She wore a black pelisse of bombasine trimmed with abundant silk embroidery, and as she surveyed Arabella from head to foot, the look in her dark eyes was arctic in the extreme.

It was all Arabella could do not to turn and run down the hall shrieking for her life in the face of such a look, particularly when Mrs. Blackwater-Younge raised a quizzing glass to her eye and inspected Arbella with a dreadful thoroughness.

"H-how do you do?" Arabella asked in a quavering voice.

"I do very well, thank you!" the other lady replied, and extended her hand, allowing, as she did so, the quizzing glass to drop on its cord to her lap. Arabella took the black glove that was offered her, and was surprised to find that Mrs. Blackwater-Younge's grip was firm and businesslike.

"You are a great deal younger than I expected," she said.

"And you are a great deal older," Arabella replied. Then, realising her faux pas, she pressed a hand to her mouth, staring at the other lady in horror.

Instead of the strong set-down she expected, this remark had the effect of causing a melting in that arctic expression, and Mrs. Blackwater's thin face creased into laughter. "Very well done!" she cried. "Very well done indeed! I deserved that, I fear! Please, do sit down. It is a great deal too bad that Rondo could not have heard you give me that set-down, for he says that I am frequently in need of one! Rondo is my husband, you see." She patted the leather sofa upon which she was seated and Arabella sank down warily beside her.

"I am your sister-in-law, Charlotte Blackwater-Younge, and you are Arabella Ivers—that is to say, you *were* Arabella Ivers until my brother took it into his head to marry you yesterday, or so my cousin Paul tells me!"

Arabella inclined her head. "The circumstances *were* unusual," she admitted.

"So like Beast," Charlotte Blackwater-Younge said

with a sigh. "Of course, he would never dream of letting one know that he had gotten married. Indeed, I had to find out he had returned from the Americas from that dreadful gossip Sally Jersey. And to think I am almost the only member of the family who is still speaking to him! I swear, after this, I may not! But you are, I believe, Margaret Tallant's child. Margaret and I came out in the same year. Oh, she was a lovely girl, everyone liked her, you know. And you do look like her, now that I see you clearly."

"M-my mother was said to be a great beauty. I fear I am not," Arabella stammered. "But I thank you for the compliment."

"Nonsense! I do not hand out compliments! Ask anyone! None of the Blackwaters do, you know. We are all insufferably arrogant," she added proudly. "Only ask Rondo, and he will tell you. Yes, I think my brother has done well in looks with his second wife. But the circumstances, my dear, seem most unusual. You do understand, of course, that Beast had to marry to gain his fortune? Not, of course, that he had no money before—my mother provided for both of us handsomely. But then I do understand that you are Sir Bosworth Ivers's oldest? Yes, of course I know your stepmother, vaguely. A most—*interesting* woman. Well, no need to tell me, my dear, one only has to know Lady Ivers to understand exactly how it all was! I hope I do not offend you—Rondo says that my tongue shall be my downfall, but you do understand that there will be gossip."

"I had not thought about that. There has been so much gossip connected with my family—Papa, you see, is not always quite beforehand with the world, and—and my stepmother . . ." Arabella bit her tongue and looked down at her hands.

"Quite so, my dear. But one only has to look at you to

know that you will fulfill the terms of dear Papa's will most perfectly for Beast. You are a lady, of course, and you are of the utmost respectability. Both the Tallants and the Ivers are old families, well known to all."

"Even if we are fallen upon hard times and reduced to shabby gentility," Arabella said dryly.

Charlotte raised her eyebrows. "I didn't say that, you did. And it don't signify in the least. Only fancy, seeing this old pile actually being cleaned out after all these years. And Fishbank likes you; that's important, you know, for Fishbank is a man who may not be trusted. Born on the estate, you know. Now, if only m'brother don't do something stupid, I imagine you'll be all right, as far as things go. Believe me, these marriages of convenience are for the best. Why, I barely knew Rondo when we were married; it was all more or less arranged by his parents and Papa, and now, you know, why I positively dote upon the man! And despite what you may hear, m'brother's not a bad sort, as long as you don't rouse his temper. Truth to tell, his first wife was a love match, and you know how *that* ended! If Beast hadn't been so pigheaded, he wouldn't have found himself in this mess in the first place! Oh, but he's good to his women, in his own way. You'll never hear him scrabbling about the bills, nor casting a block in your way, as long as you're discreet about things."

Arabella gave her such a blank look that Charlotte began to wonder if this was, indeed, a daughter of Sir Bosworth Ivers's. As enlightenment dawned upon Arabella she flushed, and Mrs. Blackwater-Younge patted her hand.

"There, there. It's a great shame you've no proper mother to advise you about these things, and I doubt that Lady Ivers—well!"

"My stepmother—indeed, no one in my family has communicated with me since I left Half Moon Street at three o'clock in the morning!" Arabella exclaimed, and allowed the whole story to pour out upon this sympathetic, if somewhat eccentric lady.

She had just finished when Fishbank came in bearing a polished silver tray holding a decanter of Madeira and a plate of macaroons. Mrs. Blackwater-Younge was forced to accept a glass of wine to fortify herself.

"Dear me! My brother is even madder than I thought!" she mused, sipping the sweetish beverage and then pouring herself more. "Of course, he always was one to run his fences. But you, my dear, well, I can't say I blame you. Only suppose that Beast were the sort of man who could offer you violence?"

"Even that would be better! At least I could fight back!" Arabella cried. "But he is not! He has been everything that is good to me, so far! Today he bought me an entire new wardrobe of clothes, and he said I might have anything I wished. Although he was angry this morning, when he saw me come in from the market with a basket on my arm."

"Dear me!" Mrs. Blackwater-Younge exclaimed, suppressing a laugh. "A market basket! Only fancy Barbara so! Well, you must never do that, not ever again, I assure you. The thing is, what are we going to do with you? If only I were out of these dreadful black gloves, but we are still in mourning for one of Rondo's aunts, you see, a perfectly dreadful old trout, and one I could never warm up to, lived in Bath and kept hundreds of cats! Ugh! But it does keep Rondo and I out of the social swim, you see, at least until Christmas, and then Town is dead. I could never understand why the London season is in the summer and the country season in the winter. One misses all the benefits of both that way, don't you think? But perhaps that will work to our advantage. By next spring, I think that they will all have some other on dit to discuss. Drat this mourning, though! Already spent six months without any balls or parties, and dead it has been, too, considering that Rondo's Aunt Hatton and I thoroughly detested each other. Didn't like Rondo, either, and everyone likes Rondo, even Beast, and he dislikes *everyone*, don't you know. Never saw such a difficult man. Of course all the Blackwaters are difficult—it runs in the blood. However, that don't signify, save that Beast won't make the least push to get you into Society; too lazy."

"I am not at all certain that I would wish to push into Society, Mrs.Blackwater-Younge—Charlotte. My deb year was a nightmare for me."

"First seasons are a nightmare for everyone. Daresay you didn't take. Daresay that woman didn't make the least push to see that you did take. Only have to see her dragging those daughters of hers about, pushing them into everyone's face, to know what that must be like. Pour me another glass of Madeira, my dear. I must think, so don't say a word."

Arabella rather anxiously did as she was told, and Mrs. Blackwater-Younge closed her eyes and screwed up her face very tightly. Clearly, thinking was an effort for her.

"I think I have a solution," she said at last, and took a healthy gulp of her wine. "We shall, that is, I shall put out the word that yours was an arrangement inspired by me! Friend of your late mother and all of that. Desired a quiet wedding because—because—" she tapped a black-gloved finger against her cheek. "Because of the idea that people might get that Blackwater was marrying you to get his money! Nothing simpler than the truth when all is said and done, or so Rondo says, and you must know that Rondo is always right!"

"I suppose that should satisfy the curious," Arabella

agreed, taking a macaroon. "Oh, dear, is it really such a scandal?"

"Scandal? Scandal? Bein' used as payment for a gaming debt by your father, sold, as it were, and there is no better word for it, to m'brother? Come now, child; if that is not scandalbroth, I don't know what is. And Beast has had far too many scandals attached to his name. No need to tarnish your own, you know."

"No, I suppose not," Arabella admitted. "Dear me, I had not considered that a private contract between two people both past their youth should cause such a commotion!"

"It would if the truth leaked out! Depend on me, it won't. Shall say yours was a whirlwind courtship, although I think your papa and your stepmama ought to be horsewhipped, the pair of them, for letting you go off in the night with Beast."

"I have two stepsisters at home who are just out, you see. We had lost all hope of my ever contracting any sort of alliance at all."

"Seen those stepsisters of your. Bracket-faced, the pair of them, and the youngest one's got spots! She'll press whom she dares, but she'll never get 'em into Almack's, no matter how hard she tries. Did you have vouchers in your deb days?"

Arabella shook her head. "Above my touch," she admitted.

"Daresay I could pull a string or two there. Princess Lieven owes me a favour. Presented at court?"

"Before the old Queen died, yes."

"Well, that's a good thing. Considering how much Prinny has won from your father at cards, that was the least he could have done, I daresay. But that can't be helped." She nodded. "Well, that spares us from having to trick up in hoops and feathers, at least. Ghastly! Went through that with all three of my girls and swore I'd never do it again. But I married 'em all off, well and happily, so there you have it, and that is more than your stepmother can say."

"Do I detect dislike between you and my stepmother?" Arabella asked frankly.

She was rewarded with a smile that softened Mrs. Blackwater-Younge's dark countenance. "Doesn't do to set *my* back up, my dear. Rondo says the Blackwaters are like the Bourbons: they learn nothing and forgive nothing! Well, be that as it may, I like you, and what's more, black gloves or no, I'm going to give you a push, enough to get you started, at least, and then you may find your own direction. Heaven knows Beast won't, but then men don't care for Society. Rondo don't either, though he likes it well enough when I arrange everything for him to be pleasant and comfortable. You may leave it to me." She smiled and patted Arabella's arm as she rose to take her leave. "Meanwhile, I'll tell you it's good to see this old place cleaned out again. I hope with a new mistress in charge, it will be as grand as it was when I was a girl here. Oh, how this house used to ring with people! Music and laughter! Well, there was Barbara, she was no hostess, though, and less of a housekeeper! Could write your name on the tables in the dust in her day, poor thing. Well, that's over and done with, and I daresay it's for the better. She would have made bad old bones, I fear. Women like her never age well, nor do they ever take it well when they do age. Dear me, Rondo will be wondering what happened to me! Call upon us in Upper Mount Street some morning. Rondo will be pleased to meet you. Meanwhile I'll be thinking, and I'll let you know what I have decided to do!"

"Yes, ma'am," Arabella said, feeling as if she had been bowled over, as much from the sheer force of Mrs.

70

Blackwater-Younge's personality as by her sister-in-law's plans for her future.

A dry kiss was planted on her cheek, and the scent of lavender lingered in her nostrils. "Don't bother to show me out—if anyone knows the way, I do. We shall speak again very soon!"

And with that she was gone.

Arabella whistled in a most unladylike manner after the door had closed upon her sister-in-law, and collapsed into a chair, downing her glass of wine.

She was still sitting there when Beast came into the room some time later, a most astonished expression on his face.

"Wife," he announced in tones of awe, "I just passed my sister on the stairs. How did you do it? She said to me, and I quote, 'Finally, Beast, you have a wife of whom I can approve. A capital sort of gel in every way. Try to keep her!' My sister, I should have warned you, is a notoriously high stickler who likes no one, not even me!"

Chapter Seven

"PLEASE, MY LADY, HOLD still, do!" pleaded Eliza Stackpole around a mouthful of hairpins, as her expert fingers rolled her mistress's hair into ringlets about her face.

"I'm sorry, truly I am, Eliza, but I want everything to be perfect tonight!"

"And so it will, be, my lady, if you will but sit for a moment and stop fidgeting with that orange stick!"

Arabella sheepishly dropped her hands into her lap and meekly surrendered her head to the ministrations of her new abigail. Although they had been working together for only a little over a fortnight, they had already settled into a comfortable relationship, and slowly, Arabella, who had done for herself all her life, was allowing herself to be tended to by this puckish creature who knew precisely what she was doing, even when her mistress did not.

Like her cousin, Eliza was small and cherubic, with a ready smile and a talent for almost anything she laid a hand to. Suddenly Arabella found her clothes mended and pressed, her hair done in a variety of fashionable styles, her bedgown laid out at night, and all the little details of attending a fashionable wardrobe—such as she had recently acquired in a most Cinderella-like fashion—magically attended to by this small miracle of a maid. When she went shopping, which she did with an enjoyable frequency, Eliza accompanied her, helping her to choose everything from kid gloves to rouge pots with the practised eye of an expert.

Somehow the cleaners had finished their job, and one day she and Beast had come from a gallop in Richmond Park to find Blackwater House immaculate from cellar to attic. Furniture gleamed with lemon oil, gilt glittered softly in the sunlight, old tapestries shone with colour and silver gleamed, divested of years of tarnish. After interviewing a steady procession of applicants from the registry office, she and Fishbank had assembled a staff that seemed to function smoothly beneath his direction. Tradesmen came with samples of brocade and velvet to replace the rotting curtains and chair covers. A French chef, temperamental with genius and the ability to tempt my lord's picky appetite, reigned by terror and brilliance belowstairs, presenting each day's menu to my lady as if he were bearing a gift of extraordinary value.

To my lady it was worth it; Beast had lost some of his cadaverous look, and once or twice had actually inquired as to mealtimes. If he was gone sometimes upon his business, Arabella had so much of her own in those days that she never questioned him about what he might be doing. In public and in private, Beast was polite to her, and sometimes amused. If he flung a rare word or two of praise at her head, for her riding ability or for the way in which she caused his house to be set and run like a clock, she cherished this as a sign that she was doing her part to keep the bargain. Since she had no social life of her own, or indeed any friends from her past life who might be counted upon to call on her now that she was Lady Blackwater, she gave him no cause for complaint.

Since she had been in the habit of directing things for so long on Half Moon Street, it did not occur to her that it should be any different in her own establishment, and a great portion of her time was devoted to setting to rights the long-neglected and overrun rooms of Blackwater House, simply as a matter of course.

Nothing could have delighted her more, not even an ermine tippet, than the bay mare Beast brought home from Tattersall's for her to ride in the park, and she looked forward to accompanying him for a gallop each day after breakfast upon Athena, whom she named after one of the heroines of Miss Webb's novels. Astride his black Arabian gelding, Beast would race her neck and neck, and they stood out against the docile and more fashionable set that plied Hyde Park in the fashionable hours. In addition he furnished the stable, adding a high-perch phaeton and matched greys for himself and a barouche for Arabella, and taking it upon himself to hire the grooms and the coachmen down from his estates in Norfolk. In the matter of horses and transport, they agreed themselves quite content, and spoke of planning to hunt in the year to come in a vague and general sort of way, as people who plan to spend time together will. Since Beast was regaining his orientation in London after years of being Abroad, and Arabella had never really had one, save for that agonizing year when she came out, they remained undisturbed by exterior forces for a halcyon period.

Happily too, since everything proceeded smoothly (and Arabella took pains to see that it did), Beast's temper remained sanguine, as it was wont to do when not provoked. If the connecting door between their bedrooms remained firmly closed. Arabella regretted it, but dared not complain. An agreement, after all, had been made.

Beneath an ancient tapestry in a corner of the ballroom, one of the workmen unearthed an ancient pianoforte, and Arabella, delighted, sent for the man to come and tune it. She set it up in a corner of the library she had adopted as her favourite chamber in the house.

Her pianoforte had been one of the first things to go during Papa's financial crisis following her debut (besides, her stepmother had said, music gave her sick headaches), and along with her horse, Arabella had missed the solace of her music. Now she set to practising in the evenings, after dinner, when her husband was having a look-in at Boodles or one of his other haunts, her rusty fingers soon flexing again as she recalled the Mozart she had loved so much years ago.

She was picking out the piano part of the second movement of Piano Concert in D Minor on one such evening when Beast came unexpectedly into the room, holding a sheet of foolscap in his hand. He opened his mouth, then closed it again, and silently leaned against the door jamb, listening to her play. He watched the look of concentration on her face as her fingers danced over the keyboard and, lost in the music, she swayed slightly from side to side.

She was, he reflected, full of surprises and hidden talents, and again he was stirred by how very little he knew about his wagered wife, and by how many surprises she could present him with in the course of the day. Certainly her inbred domestic senses were a welcome relief after so many years abroad, so much of his life spent in tents and rude inns, and before that in a sort of never-ending party that had characterized his first marriage. Watching her play the piano, Beast almost felt a fondness for her that could have been the faint stirring of love in a lesser man, but he managed to suppress the feeling.

She ran through the trills and the arpeggios with ease, throwing her shoulders forward as she haunched over the more abstract portions of the third movement, so that he could almost hear the strings and the wind of a full orchestra backing her.

It was a wonderful piece, and it made him think how much he missed music as a part of his life. There had been a time when he had held a box at the opera as well as season seats at the Academy of Ancient Music and the Concert Hall. But Barbara had detested the opera, unless she had a new gown or a new jewel to show off, and had vastly preferred the theatre—the lower and more comically vulgar the bill, the better.

He closed his eyes and let the music wash over him, feeling it soothe a restlessness in his soul, emptying him of ancient worry and replacing it with a richness of sensation, as she played through the *allegro assai* of the rondo. It was a piece that stood on its own, he thought, and really did not need the backing of an orchestra any more than a beautiful young woman needs the sparkle of diamonds; as Arabella played it, he could *see* the clarity of the piece within some mind's eye that was stimulated by the sound of music. Unbeknownst to Beast a small, faint smile had settled in his features, as light as a butterfly's wings, transforming his harsh countenance into a gentleness rarely seen there.

"*Don Giovanni,*" he whispered to himself, hearing echoes of that favourite opera in this piece.

Arabella looked up, startled, but he waved her on.

"No, no, don't stop, please," Beast commanded, and she did not, however surprised she may have been to see him standing there. Her equestrian skills may have been schooled into her, but her talent and love for music was innate. Encouraged, her fingers continued to dance on the keys, enjoying this performance enormously for the pleasure of watching the audience's reaction. She had never seen her husband so entranced, even in his most unguarded moments hithertofore, and instinctively she realized she could keep him enthralled in the spell of the music for as long as she could play.

When she had struck the last chord, she looked down at her hands as if wondering where the music had come from, and was gratified when her husband applauded her.

"Brava! Brava! Wife, you are like an Advent calendar; one never knows from day to day what one will find when one peels up the little window! Mozart!"

"I realise he is sadly out of fashion, but I do so like his work," Arabella said, flexing her fingers. "Even if I seem to do him little justice."

"Better Mozart than the tinkling little ballads most females are taught to pound out! I can remember my sister, sitting in the ballroom day after day, pounding out some weary little piece with one eye on the clock and the other on her music master!"

"This is a wonderful instrument. Italian, I assume," Arabella said, closing the lid.

"My grandfather, the Italiamaniac, brought it back from his sojourns there. If he could have known the associations that country would have with his grandson— but never mind! I came in to read you the draft of our marriage announcement m' sister insists I *must* send to the *Post* if we are to be considered really and truly legally wed. But you put me in mind that I read somewhere that there would be a performance of *Don Giovanni* at the opera—

one of the last performances of the season. Would you like to go?"

"Oh, yes!" Arabella replied, breathing like a child who has been offered a matinee at Astley's Amphitheatre by a favorite uncle. "*Very* much! Thank you!"

Beast nodded, pleased. "I shall endeavour to have Fishbank procure us a box, then. Pray, wife, play something else." With a sigh, he settled into a chair by the fire, having all the appearance of a man who means to spend the evening by his own hearth, which pleased Arabella very much indeed. Sometimes not even reading and music and endless pattern books could keep her from feeling lonely until she heard him stumbling into the dressing room in the early morning hours. Despite the new population of servants, Blackwater House still felt empty to her at times.

And yet, bit by bit, she had begun to feel like a married lady in most respects. There was, of course, a very formal meeting with Beast's family solicitors, who harrumphed and peered at her through aged and rheumy eyes while they discussed her pedigree, as if she had been a horse or a dog. Beast had been thrown into a temper and had told them to go about their business if they could not attend to his, since there were doubtless a hundred firms in Temple Bar who would gladly handle his case in Chancery. His cousin Paul and his wife had called upon her, most properly. The bishop's wife was a flighty little thing with any number of children; she had solicited Arabella to join several charitable committees as soon as she felt settled in her life, and Arabella had agreed, thinking that perhaps Mrs. Bishop Blackwater was not as flighty as she seemed—she departed with a healthy draft for the Foundling Home from Beast. Arabella no longer hesitated when addressed as Lady Blackwater, and she had heard some of her husband's stories about Central American *bandidos* more than once with a great deal of fortitude. That their lives together had so far been bounded by the demands of an enormous house, riding in the park and mealtimes, with no real stress placed upon them by the outside world, had not yet occurred to Arabella. She only knew that she had finally found some sort of peace, a haven from the storms and outrages that had hithertofore made up her life, and she was grateful for that. That such peace was fragile, and could be tested by forces she had no way of predicting, happily did not enter into her calculations, or she might have been far less sanguine as she prepared herself for dinner and the opera with her spouse that night.

"Now, my lady," Eliza said briskly, as she draped a cashmere shawl about her mistress's shoulders and gave her skirts a final shake, "You go on, and be careful not to be playing with your hair."

Recalled to herself from her brown study, Arabella started. She looked herself over quickly in the mirror, gave the hem of her gown a little kick, thanked her abigail, and made her way down the stairs to the dining room.

He did not immediately hear her as she came into the room, and she had a chance to study him, unawares. He leaned against the ornate Lightfoot carved fireplace, the flames giving him illumination in his black evening dress relieved only by the white of his cravat and shirt. One black-stockinged leg was bent so that his foot rested on the brass fender, and his profile, as he looked down into the flames, appeared sharp and hawkish. Even in repose his features bore a harsh cast—his deep-set dark eyes shadowed by his thick, black brow, his rather thin lips set in a strong line over a determined jaw, his aquiline nose giving his countenance a classical ambience.

With a sixth sense he looked up and saw her standing in the doorway, and a slow, approving smile, like sunshine breaking out from behind the clouds, illuminated his expression. "Well done, wife!" he announced, moving toward her with both hands outstretched.

Arabella smiled in return. She knew that she was looking her best, in a gown of poppy-coloured India muslin ornamented with small sprigs of gold. The rather low corsage was banded in double rows of gold lace, and the short, puffy sleeves were encased in bands of gold to match the bodice. The wadded hem, just coming into fashion, was banded with double columns of gold lace set apart with gold rosettes. Eliza had dressed her hair *à la Russie*, smoothly parted in the middle with clusters of auburn ringlets framing her temples and cheeks and a series of large curls rolled on the crown and falling down her neck. On her feet, Arabella wore a pair of white satin slippers striped with gold, and eighteen-button kid gloves covered her hands and forearms up to just above the elbow. Over her shoulders she had draped a cashmere shawl, and about her neck she wore her only jewellery, the single strand of pearls from her mother.

It was with a sudden catch in his throat that Beast Blackwater realised he had married a beautiful woman. It was not so much the perfection of her features, nor the lustre of her skin, nor the charm of her figure—although these were there in some degree—it was the radiance that shone from her, as if she had been illuminated from inside, a light that seemed to pour out of her in this moment of happiness. In the full flower of her new confidence, her youth and her happiness, she stood before him. For a moment, Beast was speechless.

But for a moment only. Such a betrayal of emotions was alien to his nature, and he looked away from her for a fraction of a second to recover himself. Surely it would never do for one's own wife to know that one was developing a decided partiality toward her.

Seeking distraction his eye fell upon the ancient mahogany caskets lying on the table, and he cleared his throat. "Before we start dinner, there is something I have for you," he said, casually flipping open the top box. "These have been in my family for a number of years, and as the new Lady Blackwater, you will of course wish to wear them, whenever you choose."

He removed a glittering pile of diamonds and rubies and placed it upon Arabella's head. "The ruby tiara, and there is a necklace and a set of bracelets that match, somewhere. Belonged to m'mother, who had it from some French émigré, actually. But not, I think with that orange dress." He removed the tiara, and in truth Arabella was relieved, for it weighed a great deal besides digging into her head. "Well, there's your viscountess cornet and mine, all gold balls, but this is only for great state events, such as coronations and the like, and not for the opera—gold! Yes, I think we need gold! Lord, I haven't seen this tangle since Bar—since my wife died; been in a vault at the lawyers, you see! Well, then, I think *this* . . ."

Beast rooted about in the drawers of the jewel case and produced a rather elegant gold headband set with emeralds and diamonds in the shape of flowers, which he placed carefully on Arabella's head. "And this . . ." He screwed onto her lobes a pair of gold and emerald earrings made to resemble tiny vines of ivy, and dug once again among the velvet pouches. "A pair of bracelets, emerald and diamond, as you see, and the necklace—"

"It's more like a bib!" Arabella exclaimed as an enormous array of diamond and emerald flowers was held before her eyes.

"Unclasp those pearls. Tonight, you appear as Lady Blackwater!"

"Princess Charlotte herself could not feel more special than I!" Arabella exclaimed as she removed her mother's pearls and Beast replaced them with the necklace. She shivered slightly.

"Is something the matter?" Beast asked.

Arabella frowned slightly. "Only that the gold is so cold against my skin," she said, touching the center emerald, an enormous stone the size of a quail's egg and as cold as green ice beneath her fingers. She peered at herself in the mirror above the sideboard, half in wonder, half in amusement to see Sir Bosworth Ivers's daughter decked out in such a fashion.

"At your age," Beast said, coming to stand behind her, his long, thin hands on her shoulders, his face aglow with simple pride, "you do not need jewels to set you off. Youth and beauty—" Arabella flushed at the compliment, and smiled, touching her husband's hand lightly with her own, "—are quite enough. It is only when one loses that glow that jewels become absolutely necessary to give a woman that certain light. But tonight, we gild the lily, what?"

"I suppose so," Arabella said, quite nonplussed to any further speech. How heavy it all felt, and yet how much fun to see oneself bejewelled and dressed so beautifully. She turned her wrists this way and that so that the bracelets caught the light. "I wish—" she started to say, and stopped. How could she possibly wish for anything more? Had not her husband kept every part of his bargain with her? And what would she wish for? That he might love her, just a little, as she was beginning to love him? That was too much to ask for, Arabella realised. He was only trying to be kind to her, and she was responding to kindness as a dry and thirsty plant responds to rain. For him their marriage was a business arrangement only. She fulfilled the terms of his father's will, and her only other real function in his life was to produce an heir, which she was certainly willing to do whenever he expressed interest in the subject. Below those things, she wanted to make this sad man happy; somehow that seemed terribly important to her. She wanted his house to be well run, and she never, ever wanted him to feel that she in any way placed any sort of emotional demands upon him. *That* had definitely not been a part of the contract, and doubtless he would be horrified if he suspected that she regarded him with anything other than warmth and gratitude for his kindness in taking her away from Half Moon Street, in giving her this new and somewhat heady life as his viscountess.

"You wish what, wife?" Beast asked quizzically, meeting her eyes in the mirror.

For a moment she thought he might be able to read her mind through her expression as she gazed at his reflection above her head, and she dropped her eyes, embarrassed. "I wish—I wish there were some way I could repay you for all your kindness!" she managed to stammer out.

He looked puzzled for a moment. It was easy for Arabella, believing as she did that he could only regard her with a sort of pity, or at best a sense of friendship, to feel that any expression of her true emotions would have repulsed him, undermining any sense of the fragile understanding they had achieved in their short marriage. If she had known that his own feelings, unexamined but intuitively kept in check lest he frighten or intimidate her, had the potential to match her own, she might have been the happiest woman in London at that moment. But neither party possessed the talent of clairvoyance, and she merely stammered, "You have been so very good to me!"

Beast concealed his feelings with a scowl, patting her shoulder in a rather brotherly fashion. "Nonsense! As my viscountess, I expect you to make a good show. And as a lady who has done me the very great honour of rescuing me from certain misery, it is I who owe you a very great debt! Arabella, whatever you want, please, do not hesitate! A bit of jewellery, a dress, a bit of pin money to lose at cards, a high-perch phaeton—you have but to order it! I cannot forget what a very high debt I owe you, nor how gracefully you have born up under what cannot help but be very distressing circumstances! Whatever you want, it is yours! I promise I shall never cavail at your bills—or at any other *arrangements* you might wish to make!"

"Arrangements?" Arabella asked, thinking she would have traded every jewel in those boxes for just one hint that his feelings toward her were even tepidly affectionate.

He waved a languid hand in the air. "You know, arrangements! Personal matters—friendships, interests, er, entanglements, if you like. I cannot expect you to— well, once we have an heir, you are free to pursue whatever interests you!"

Arabella flushed as scarlet as the rubies tossed carelessly on the surface of the mahogany Chippendale sideboard. "I—I see," she said loosely, and began to carefully gather up the state pieces, placing them back in the box. Perhaps, she thought, this means that he wishes also to continue his arrangements with such as the Lady S———. What can I possibly say? That I have never had another man, and would never wish any other than this strange, black-mooded man with his foul temper and his great sweeping generosity? "Just as you wish," she said, closing the cases on the sparkle of jewels. "Shall we eat? The hour grows late, and I yearn for *Don Giovanni*."

Her smile felt as cold on her face as the emeralds at her neck.

Beast laughed uneasily, perhaps aware that he might have spoken too soon and too frankly. How could she know what pitfalls and intrigues lay outside the doors of Blackwater House? He knew all too well, and to his great cost. But he had lost his first wife to those tangles and snares that comprised the fashionable life in London, and he meant not to destroy his second wife with the fury of his possessive passions, his old-fashioned and decidedly bourgeois preference for fidelity. *This*, after all, was no love match but a contract of convenience. He had not the right to demand anything from Arabella other than that she conduct herself discreetly, no matter how he was beginning to feel toward his bartered bride. Eventually, of course, an heir must be produced, and certain steps must be taken to produce that effect. But for the first time in his career, Beast found himself at a loss as to how to instigate this.

Chapter Eight

ALTHOUGH IT WAS THE very end of the
Season, and town was thin of company,
the Blackwaters' coach had, perforce, to join a long line
inching toward the entrance of the Opera House to
discharge glittering passengers.

Blackwater, who had kept no regular box at the opera
in many years, had managed to borrow for the evening his
sister and brother-in-law's box, and it was to this partition
that he escorted his wife. Since Mrs. Blackwater-Younge
was one of those rare individuals who attended the opera
as much for the love of music as for the chance to see and
be seen, the location of her box was excellent, offering not
only a good view of the stage, now heavily curtained, but
also some of the best acoustics to be found within the
theatre.

Arabella was all eyes to see what went on about her as she settled into her seat and allowed Beast to remove her evening cloak and adjust her chair for a better view of the stage. Other boxes were filling with fashionably dressed people, gentlemen elegant in their black-and-white evening dress, ladies glittering in jewels and nodding with plumes. It had been many years since she had attended an opera, the present Lady Ivers being no great admirer of music and finding it an awkward place in which to expend her social-climbing skills. Arabella settled back to enjoy the evening, with a glance or two at her husband to be certain that he, too, was enjoying himself.

Rumours of the sudden and unexpected second marriage of Beast Blackwater had spread through London, and in this, their first appearance in public together, Lord and Lady Blackwater were getting more than their share of attention from the other patrons.

Beast may have noted this, and dismissed it as being of little consequence. After all, Blackwaters take little note of the rest of the world, their persons being, by their lights, quite above such worries as what opinion others might hold of them. But Arabella, with her head buried in her program and her attention equally divided between a study of the night's performers and a discussion of their relative merits with her husband, did not notice at all.

Once or twice old friends of Beast's dropped by the box, languid men with decidedly clenched drawls and the bored airs of people who might prefer to be out on the field, in the boxing ring, or at the head of a team, rather than confined in this airless, stuffy space of red and gilt, illuminated by the new gas jets. They paid their respects to his wife, coolly and with a lively interest appraising Beast's second choice behind their polite indifference, even as they spoke of the hunting season and the latest on dits in their circles. To a man, they came away pleased with the new Lady Blackwater's looks, as well as with her natural and unaffected charms; many of them begged to be allowed to call upon her as well as her husband.

"You would seem to be establishing your court, wife," Beast teased her after one particularly notable Corinthian had lingered in conversation with her for a good ten minutes before surrendering her to a waiting group.

"They are your friends," Arabella replied, a little naively, "of course I want them to feel that they may call upon us whenever they wish."

Since they had not bothered to call upon him on his return from the Americas a few months earlier, Beast hardly felt they were his friends. Rather they were his comrades from an earlier and wilder day, who, it seemed to him, had melted away at the first sign of trouble between himself and Barbara. However, he was of a mood to be expansive, and neither by a frown nor a harsh word did he discourage them in their attempts to rekindle old interests, accepting invitations to box a round or two at Jackson's, look in at White's or St. James's, or to come and inspect a bang-up piece of blood and bone they had recently purchased at a steal. Rather than being jealous of these old friends from earlier days, Arabella seemed to be anxious to encourage him to reestablish his friendships with old comrades, and he found himself wondering if she did not hope they would take him away from home and away from her more often in order that she might pursue her own diversions.

What these diversions might be, Beast could not guess, since his wife, to his knowledge, had seemed entirely preoccupied with establishing her household since their marriage. Then, when he saw no less a person than Princess Lieven beckoning to him from the opposite tier, he had a sudden and sinking feeling that his halcyon days were about to end.

"Who is that lady, the dark one in all the diamonds who is waving and smiling to us with so much determination?" Arabella asked from behind her fan.

Beast sighed. "That, wife, is Princess Lieven, wife of the Russian ambassador and one of the most formidable hostesses in London. I believe she would like to meet you, so we must go and make our respects."

"Goodness, what diamonds!"

"Gifts from the Tsar, or so I am told." Beast rose and took her hand. "Come, Lady Blackwater; the curiosity of the lady *must* be satisfied."

Arabella allowed herself to be led through the gallery to the opposite tier, where a restless, thin woman with great dark eyes sat surrounded by her entourage, smiling up at her. Those great dark eyes missed nothing, Arabella thought as she took the beringed hand offered to her and listened as her husband introduced her to this strange, shrewd-looking woman.

"So, this is the Lady Blackwater of whom all London is talking," Princess Lieven said in her excellent, if slightly gutturally accented French. "Do you see, Alexi, this is the lady. Blackwater, you are very, very bad!"

Alexi, a young and languid man who formed part of her entourage, lifted his quizzing glass to his eye and surveyed Arabella with frank admiration as Beast leaned negligently against the door of the box and grinned insolently down at the ambassadress.

"Indeed, and why do you say so, Dorothea?" he drawled.

The princess laughed, slapping his arm with a rolled-up fan. "Because you go to America—*America*! No one goes to America, save Talleyrand, and *he* stayed in a boarding house—*a boarding house!*—in Philadelphia, and should, if you ask me, still be there! *Diable en enfer!* And you do not say good-bye to your friends. And then you return, and you do not come to call upon your friends. And to make matters very sad indeed, you marry and do not tell one, but let one read the announcement in the *Post!*" She shook her head and smiled, but Arabella could tell she was displeased. "You neglect your friends, Beast! And hide such a charming wife from us all!"

"Thank you, ma'am," Beast drawled, amused by these blows raining down on his head. "I find my wife very charming!"

The dark eyes narrowed as they gazed at Arabella appraisingly. "You are Sir Bosworth's daughter, hein? And your mama was Miss Tallant. A lovely girl, I remember her well from when she would come to Almack's as a deb. Well, we do not see you at Almack's?"

"No, ma'am," Arabella said. "One does not see me anywhere. We have been setting Blackwater House to rights."

For some reason the princess found this amusing, and her laughter was like the tinkle of silver. "Do you hear, Alexi, they have been setting the house to rights! *Alors,* I think Beast merely wants to keep you all for himself, don't you Alexi—ah, Lady Blackwater, may I present Count Baransky."

"Charmed, ma'am." Count Baransky dropped his quizzing glass and bowed low. He was of an age with Arabella and quite dashingly handsome, being blond and fair with a wonderful blond mustache that curled up on the ends. He took Arabella's hand into his own and bowed low over it, holding it for just a second longer than necessary.

"Count Baransky is my cousin. He is attached to our embassy," the princess said lazily, watching this interaction with interest.

"I am most charmed to meet the beautiful Lady

Blackwater," the count repeated. "One does not encounter such beauty every day."

Arabella gently disengaged her hand from his and looked at her husband, who was frowning dangerously at the Russian gentleman.

"Well," he said, "wife, I suppose we should be getting back to our box."

"You will call on me, I hope?" the princess asked, smiling at Arabella.

"Yes, ma'am," Arabella said. "I think I should enjoy that." She was intrigued by the princess, who was said to have one of the best political minds in Europe.

"Beast!" drawled a strange voice, and everyone turned at once to look.

Even if she had not seen that Cruikshank caricature, Arabella would have known the woman at once, for she was wearing the jonquil-coloured barege dress that Arabella had so admired at Madam Celeste's. About her neck hung a veritable chandelier of diamonds, and the look on her pretty, proud face was haughty enough to freeze ice. This, then, was Lady S———, Arabella thought, and was considering the great feeling of jealousy that washed over her.

Beneath sleepy lids, Princess Lieven's eyes flickered with attention as she watched this most interesting meeting. She was herself a worldly and sophisticated woman who had tolerated her own husband's numerous infidelities with understanding. She was slightly amused by the most English flush that flew into Arabella's cheeks, and by the cool, appraising look that Lady Sibley cast over her lover's new wife. She only raised an eyebrow over the look of absolute fury that passed across Beast Blackwater's face when he beheld his mistress confronting his wife.

Lady Sibley was well above the medium height, and somewhere in her early thirties. The blond of her hair may have been aided by tinting, but nothing other than nature could have given her such intensely blue eyes. Her prettiness was tempered, though, by a certain hardness about the set of her lips and the calculating look in her eyes. She stood for a moment between the curtains, posing for the inhabitants of the box, one hand spreading her fan and the other touching the diamonds that sparkled about her neck, smiling a smile that never reached her eyes.

"My dear princess," she purred in careful accents, as if the tongue of the Upper Ten Thousand were not what she had been raised to speak. "I saw you, and knew that Sibley and I must come and pay our respects to you at once! My husband is on his way, but his gout is unusually ferocious tonight, I fear. Ah, Blackwater! It seems an age since last we met! How do you do?"

Blackwater's frown was very black indeed as he brushed a hand against the languid glove that was extended to him. "I thought I had made that clear to you," he said stiffly, and his eyes flashed a secret message of rage.

But Lady Sibley chose to ignore these storm warnings as she turned toward Arabella, looking at her as if seeing her for the first time. "And this," she purred, "must be the newest Lady Blackwater. Enchanted, I am certain."

Arabella nodded stiffly, willing the flush to leave her face. Still, she could not help but study the woman who was her husband's mistress—barege dress, diamonds and all. There was something overwhelming about her, Arabella thought, something musky and erotic that she instinctively distrusted and despised. "I would have known you anywhere," Arabella heard herself saying, determined not to be intimidated by this fashionable, sensual creature, whom she recognized at once as an enemy—and a formidable one at that. "You see, I saw a caricature of your necklace."

Princess Lieven stifled a giggle. Cold sparks flashed in

Lady Sibley's eyes, but her smile remained frozen on her hard and lovely face as she furled her fan and tapped Arabella on the arm. "I am often caricatured," she said lightly. "But never ever imitated. You must ask your husband about that."

Beast stirred slightly, and Arabella felt him stiffen. She tilted her chin upward. "Really, I cannot wonder, ma'am," she replied coolly, "for who would want to imitate an imitation?"

Princess Lieven actually smiled openly, showing her teeth. Count Baransky twirled his mustaches to conceal his smile, and a young lady opened her fan to hide a gasp.

Lady Sibley's hand tightened about the fan until the thinly carved ivory sticks snapped, but her expression did not change. At that moment, Arabella knew she would neither forget nor forgive, and that she would not miss an opportunity to revenge herself on Arabella.

"Ho, ho, here I find you, my dear," boomed a voice behind her at that moment, and an elderly man, his enormous belly flowing out from a vast and embroidered waistcoat, his jowly face flushed to the colour of port, appeared in the curtains. The look with which he surveyed the box betrayed no trace of intelligence nor wit, and oblivious to the mise-en-scène, he shook a fat finger at Lady Sibley. "Here I find you, my dear," he repeated, leaning heavily on a mahogany cane, obviously pleased with himself for this discovery. "In Princess Lieven's box, what? Evening, Princess. Blackwater. Baransky. Can't recall who the rest of you are, but good evening to you all."

"May I present my wife, Lord Sibley? Arabella, this is Lord Sibley," Beast said coolly, holding back his temper with an effort as he glared at his former mistress.

The large, loose-lipped face was turned to Arabella with a vacuous curiosity, and a great deal of good nature. "Hello, my dear. Heard Beast was buckled at last! Charming! Charming!" As he bowed, his stays creaked alarmingly.

"Godolphin, I have a pressing headache," Lady Sibley said, turning away. "We must go home at once. I cannot stay here!"

"What! What? But you said—" Lord Sibley exclaimed, surprised. "Everyone here!"

"Never mind what I said! I want to go home! Now!" With those words, Lady Sibley stormed out of the box, leaving her puzzled husband to laboriously plod after her, leaning heavily on his cane.

"I shall never understand women . . ." he was heard to say, sighing.

"And I think also, wife, that we should return to our box. The curtain is about to go up, you know," Beast said, firmly taking Arabella by the arm.

She flushed, afraid to look at his face. She felt half a dozen pairs of curious eyes on her face, and did not know where to look.

"A moment, if you please," Princess Lieven said, holding out her hand to Arabella and smiling. "Please, my dear, do not forget to call upon me! I shall look forward to it!"

"As shall I," Count Baransky said, his eyes glowing.

"Of course, if you wish it," Arabella managed to stammer.

The princess laughed. "Wish it? My dear, I shall command it! Thursday at ten! We shall have a comfortable coze, you and I."

Arabella bowed. "Just as you wish."

"I shall see that she recalls it, Princess," Beast said firmly. "And now, we must bid you good evening."

"So," the princess said, laughing when they had made their exit, "the little kitten has claws enough to take on the old tabby! Lord, I thought I should burst out laughing!

Wonderful, wonderful! One never imitates an imitation! Wonderful! I shall give her Almack's vouchers!"

Beast's stride was so long that Arabella had to scurry, picking up her skirts, to keep up with him.

"I suppose," he said in tones that betrayed nothing of his real feelings, "that I owe you an apology for that disgraceful scene. An explanation?"

Arabella looked straight ahead. "No explanation is necessary," she replied. "After all, that was not a part of our arrangement, was it?"

"Our arrangement. Yes, I am forgetting," Beast said, stepping aside to allow her to enter the velvet-draped box. "We have an arrangement, do we not? Nonetheless, I assure you it will never happen again."

She could not bring herself to look at his face. He would be, she was certain, full of rage for the way in which she had insulted his mistress. When he said it would never happen again, she chose to read this as a command, and lowered her head to her program to conceal her blushes.

Beast, watching her reaction, was stabbed in the heart to think that Lady Sibley's outrageous, vulgar behaviour had wounded her so that she would not even bring herself to look at him. He yearned to reach over and take her hand, to apologise for subjecting her to such an ordeal, but he drew back, certain that she would reject him coldly. The barege dress had been his parting present to his ladylove upon his marriage to another; at the time, he had believed Caroline's experience in these matters, which was considerable, would have led her to understand that the tête-à-tête the week after Arabella's visit to Mme Celeste had been their last. He had not counted upon her indiscretion, nor her wounded vanity allowing her to make such a fool of herself before the very people whose social approval she so desperately craved. Never, ever would Caroline Sibley be offered vouchers to Almack's by Princess Lieven or by cess Lieven or by any of its other patronesses; her background was far too well known. For the first time he realised the levels of rage and jealousy that dwelt in that perfumed bosom, and he shuddered, glad to be rid of her and her predatory, greedy ways.

He glanced at the woman he had made his wife, and was surprised at the affection he felt toward her, and yes, pride in the way she had squelched Lady Sibley's insults. He was about to lean over and whisper something of that into her ear, but at that moment the curtain came up on *Don Giovanni*, and for the next three hours she was lost to him and to all the world but that of Mozart.

Not, however, Princess Lieven. Opera bored her; she came only to see and be seen and to mingle with her friends. Concealing a yawn behind her fan, she leaned back to speak to Count Baransky behind her. "So, the new Lady Blackwater is not such a mouse as everyone says! I doubt very much this story of a long and hidden attachment, but she has a certain beauty behind those freckles, and the wit to depress Caroline Sibley's odiousness! It might be amusing to make her fashionable, do you not think? Perhaps then her husband will appreciate her charms."

"If he does not, I do!" Count Baransky said reverently. "She is a goddess!"

"Romantic boy," his cousin said, sighing indulgently, and returned to studying the jewels present that night.

Chapter Nine

"PRINCESS LIEVEN! YOU CALLED on her, I hope?"

"Oh, yes. Beast said I must, that she was very powerful and could make or break me socially, which seems to matter a great deal to him. He seems to think it should make me happy. But yes, I went to the residence, on Grosvenor Square, and you should see—"

"But my dear Arabella, I have seen. All velvet and gold and very grand butlers and majordomos and Russian plate. Catherine the Great furnished the place, you know—all that wonderful Russian furniture sent from St. Petersburg but done by French craftsmen, of course. And she was at home?" Mrs. Blackwater-Younge asked.

"Very much so, in the vastest morning dress I ever saw, yards and yards and yards of ruffles and lace and a mobcap that stood quite a good foot off her head and was tied in an enormous bow under her chin. She received me in a boudoir all done in gold and crimson and ermine, most amazing. She reclined on a chaise the entire visit, surrounded by little yappy dogs, and drank chocolate and ate almond paste, asking me the oddest questions all the while."

"Questions?"

"Oh, you know, the usual everyone asks. About my mother and my father and my stepmother and my marriage, and you, of course. She rather worked the conversation around to what I knew about Lady Sibley, and then told me the most awful stories about her starting out life as an employee of Harriette Wilson's establishment and marrying Lord Sibley for his money, of which he seems to have a great deal, and *all* her lovers. You would have thought me a wilting deb, she was so delicate about it all."

"I daresay she was trying to be kind; that is Alexa's way, you know, trying to warn you. Never mind, no one with the least pretension to ton will admit Caroline Sibley *anywhere*, least of all Almack's, so you need not fear her again."

"I wonder. I imagine she can be a formidable enemy. The princess says she prefers to cast off her lovers, rather than to have them cast her away."

"She don't signify, I assure you, my dear. Why, even Rondo has had his little flings, and he is devoted to me, and I to him."

"Oh no, it's different between Beast and I. Our arrangement—"

"Oh, I assure you, he'll survive the ordeal, and see the light, if he hasn't already. Men like to be comfortable, my dear, and I doubt that Caroline Sibley knows how to make a man comfortable, whatever other tricks she may have up her sleeve. But do go on!"

"That was Thursday. On Friday, just as I was about to go off with Beast to ride in Richmond Park, Count Baransky appeared on the doorstep. What could I do? I had to see him. He wore his hussar uniform and lolled about the drawing room, twirling his mustaches and gazing at me in the most idiotic way. At first I thought he was quite unwell, but then he read a poem he had composed about my freckles, and I didn't know where to look! Happily Fishbank appeared out of nowhere, the way he does when you need him, and said there was a crisis in the housekeeping room and I must come immediately, so the count of course had to take his leave."

"A veritable Adonis! I have seen him! As a ciscebeo, he will do you credit."

"I suppose so, but when Beast comes upon him in the house, he growls and leaves immediately, saying he cannot bear a man-milliner underfoot."

"Every lady of fashion is entitled to her ciscebeos, of course," Mrs. Blackwater-Young said. "He cannot possibly object to Baransky. His ton is of the highest! His cousin is the Tsar, you know, and he was a hero in some campaign or another against Bonaparte."

"Well, he ought to find a nice Yorkshire heiress and get married and have some children," Arabella said, sighing, "instead of living in my drawing room and writing bad poetry. He dances very well, though."

"Almack's on Tuesday?"

"Yes, and Beast refuses flat out to go, so it had to be Baransky. It hasn't changed since my deb days. Cold rooms, warm punch and a flock of very silly girls all mooning over Baransky, for which I do not blame them—I blame him for not taking an interest in any of them!"

"And you, I suppose, encouraged him to wait upon these die-away debutantes?"

"Of course. But he won't hear of it, which quite annoys me. And then, of course, Mrs. Drummond-Burrell and Sally Jersey paid a morning call, one of them so stiff and grand, the other flittering all over the room. I am invited to Sally's ball. Beast must go to that, even if he doesn't want to; he has known Sally forever."

"I am afraid it will have to be Count Baransky again," Mrs. Blackwater-Younge said with a sigh. "There is a horrid mill they are all going to see on Friday, even my Rondo. I cannot understand what pleasure men derive from watching two other men pummel each other into raw meat, but there you have it."

"Then Beast must go; I won't even mention Sally to him," Arabella said firmly. "He does love boxing, you see. He goes to Jackson's every day he can for at least an hour. I couldn't deprive him of that pleasure; it would be so unfair, when he would much rather be at a mill than a ball."

"Spoken with rare understanding!" Mrs. Blackwater-Younge exclaimed. "My brother is luckier than he knows, to have a wife so understanding."

"I try to see that he can do just as he likes," Arabella replied, "and try not to tease him with things he doesn't much care for. It only seems fair, you know."

"If I let Rondo do just as he liked, there *would* be a rare time. As long as you arrange everything for them, and don't plague them too much about the details, men are happy enough to go with you."

"We did go to a concert of ancient music the other night. We both like music, you see. And there is Lady Bridgeton's ball, of course."

"He must attend that with you, at all counts! Rondo hates such things too, but he can generally find someone to play cards with him, and that helps."

Arabella smiled thinly. "I doubt that my husband will ever want to play cards again," she said softly.

"Of course," her sister-in-law replied, laughing gently, "I am forgetting. But if all his games of chance came out as well as you, I should drive him to Waitier's every night!"

"You are kind to me," Arabella said, smiling. "Dearest Charlotte, what would I do without you?"

"Drat these black gloves!" Mrs. Blackwater-Younge said with a sigh, pulling on them as they lay in her lap. "It would be so much simpler if I could launch you properly, give a ball for you and all of that, take you about to leave your cards, introduce you to the right people. Beast has no idea of these things, and what's more he doesn't care."

"Nor would I, really, if it did not seem so important to him that I become fashionable. Indeed, it would seem that I am become so fashionable of late that I rarely get to spend any time at all with my husband. We always seem to be bound upon different errands, passing on the front step. This business of being fashionable certainly is time consuming."

"Dull business indeed!"

The two ladies were circling Hyde Park in Arabella's new high-perch phaeton with its distinctive red-rimmed wheels, drawn by a set of matched greys, a wedding present from her solvent husband. Moving through the ceaseless throng of fashionable drivers at the snail's pace her sister-in-law preferred, Arabella found such outings a trifle tedious, yearning as she did for Richmond Park at an unfashionable hour in which to give the team their full head and gallop. But, as this outing, like many others, was designed to show the Polite World that the new Lady Blackwater enjoyed the full approval of her socially powerful sister-in-law, as well as to allow Charlotte to escape, for a while, the deadly dull confines of her mourning period, Arabella tolerated it. Besides, she was very fond of her outspoken sister-in-law and would not have hurt her feelings for all the world. Her company, like her brother's, was never boring to Arabella.

"How are you and Beast coming along?" Mrs. Blackwater-Younge asked, nodding grandly to some passing friends in a barouche.

Arabella looked down at her hands, gloved in York tan. "Well enough. He has his interests and I have mine, of course. But we are—compatible!"

"But," Mrs. Blackwater-Younge said, and waited.

Arabella forced herself to smile as she nodded and bowed to two gentlemen on horseback. "I cannot seem to—that is, I would like very much to—well, we would like a child. And Blackwater must have an heir." She bit her lower lip, at a loss for words.

Mrs. Blackwater-Younge laughed, placing a hand on Arabella's wrist. "My dear girl, you have only been married for about six weeks, if I collect right!"

"Even so, I—"

"Rondo and I thought we should never have a child. But now we have four, and if you do not count poor Maria, who died in infancy, that is a very good number. It is simply a matter of time, my dear, and then you will wonder why you ever worried about such things. In fact, you will start to worry about quite the opposite, but we shall deal with that when that time comes!"

"I do so hope for a child," Arabella said, sighing. "It might—it might bring us closer together."

Charlotte laughed. "What a very droll notion! Arabella, are you possibly falling in love with your husband?"

Arabella pulled on the reins a little harder than she intended, and quickly righted her fingering. "What a very odd idea, to be sure," she said with a laugh. "Beast is determined that I shall be fashionable, and you know that a lady of fashion is in love with anyone but her husband!"

"Nonetheless, my dear, whenever you speak about Beast, I detect a decided partiality in your tone of voice! I admit that I quite dote upon Rondo, but it was not so when we married, I assure you! Dear me, what a rough row you have chosen, Arabella! My brother has a heart of cold, grey stone."

Arabella opened her mouth to protest, but at that moment they were hailed by no less a person than Princess Lieven herself, drawn through the park in a fashionable barouche, with footmen before and behind, and Count Baransky seated beside her.

"Ah, the Blackwater ladies, and so charming you both look!" the princess drawled in her husky accents as the two carriages drew side by side. "Charlotte, it seems an age since last I saw you! Arabella, do you mind if I borrow your sister-in-law for a turn about the park? So much gossiping we two middle-aged harridans have to do! You may take Baransky, and we shall meet by the gate."

With considerable assistance from the princess's footmen (she never travelled without at least four), this exchange was accomplished, and Arabella soon found herself resuming her trot around the row, the young Russian count beside her.

He was, she had to admit, looking very handsome in his hussar uniform with its cape and green and scarlet trimmings, and his mustache seemed in particularly fine fettle today, curling up on either side of his lip in a smile. Not for the first time, Arabella wished he did not smell so strongly of cologne. She thought about how Beast smelled; of clean linen and a certain masculine soap, no more than a breath upon the senses.

"It is a lovely day," the young count said, sighing and leaning back against the leather squabs while watching with admiration as Arabella threaded her phaeton between a lumbering landaulet and a barouche. "And you are looking so soignée, Lady Blackwater, in your little toque. Is that the lastest style from Paris?"

Arabella smiled, appreciating his compliments. She did feel that she looked smart in her driving drag of dove-grey merino trimmed with white silk braid, a little felt cap adjusted at a rakish angle over her curls by the faithful Eliza, its white plumes bobbing over her cheek. "I think it must be, for my maid assures me that to be without one is to be a dowd. And what have you been doing since last we met?"

"Ah," Baransky said with a sigh, reaching into his tunic. "I have been composing poetry. You will permit me to read an ode, in English, upon your eyes?"

"I see Miss Elverson and her mother, nodding and waving to you, over there," Arabella said, as much to recall him to his manners as to avoid yet another encounter with the count's excessively tedious attempts at verse.

Rather firmly, she drew up beside the young lady and her mother, and pointedly opened the conversation by complimenting Miss Elverson on her appreciation for the literary arts. Alas, not even five minutes' conversation with the prettiest debutante of the season managed to distract the count from his determination to share his latest work with any who would hear it; Arabella bit her lip and tried to conceal her impatience as a very derivative bit of doggerel was recited aloud, concerning her eyes and her freckles.

Miss Elverson, like every other young lady in London, was open in her admiration of the handsome Russian, and so entirely uncritical of his efforts to become the next Byron that Arabella, who was ordinarily quite fond of the girl, had a strong urge to shake her by the time they had bid the ladies a civil good day and gone upon their way.

"You see?" the count asked mournfully, turning his enormous and expressive blue eyes upon Arabella with great sadness, "Miss Elverson thinks I am a fine poet, even in English."

"And Miss Elverson is a remarkably praiseworthy young woman," Arabella replied. "Certainly, the man who manages to catch her interest will be lucky indeed."

Baransky could only shrug. "Sometimes, I think you wish I would marry," he said.

"Of course I wish you would marry," Arabella replied. "Marriage is a very agreeable state, you know."

"Then I would be disloyal to you, for whom I have conceived a hopeless passion," Baransky said mournfully, enjoying himself thoroughly. A true romantic must of course have a hopeless passion in order to inspire himself to the heights of suffering for his art. And that Season, the young count had found the guise of a romantic poet to be most fashionable indeed, particularly now that he fancied himself deeply in love with an unattainable lady. It was perhaps unfortunate that the unattainable lady for whom he had developed an attachment had a rather prosaic habit of depressing his pretensions to unrequited devotion, but Arabella was fashionable, and he could not conceive of developing a hopeless attachment to a lady who was not in the very first stare of ton. Still, he could not resist adding, "Anyway, from what I see of your marriage to Beast, marriage is not such a wonderful state of affairs, after all. You go your way and he goes his, and he has Lady Sibley, although she is not such good ton."

Although this was meant to taunt her for not adhering to the rules of unrequited passion, Arabella took it seriously, wondering if he knew something she did not. However, her pride as well as her manners forbade her to pursue the subject. Baransky, oblivious to the havoc he caused within her bosom, turned the subject to a forthcoming ball he would be escorting her to and allowed the matter to drop, satisfied that he had established his devotion for the day.

Not for the entire world would Baransky deliberately have hurt the Unattainable, as he thought of Arabella. Certainly he would have been very much distressed had he known that a languid and petulant remark, without any foundation known to him to be true, had caused Arabella to doubt that the liaison between Beast and the venial countess was ended. Not only would he have been horrified to know he had hurt such a good friend and lady of fashion, but it would also have been extremely bad ton. And the Russian count never wanted to be louche; the very idea was horrifying.

And besides consideration for his own poetic feelings, there was also the very uneasy consideration that should the marriage of the Unattainable and her philistine husband fall apart, the lady might seek consolation from him. As much as the count adored Arabella, he certainly did not wish for *that*. He was very comfortable in his bachelor existence, after all, and his own private arrangement with an opera dancer, a very pretty and very stupid female, was all that he could manage with his busy social life and his poetry.

But Arabella concealed her distress behind a smile, and turned the topic to the latest on dit concerning Lord Byron, who was said to be living in Italy in a ménage à trois with an Italian countess and her complaisant husband.

"Whenever I think about countesses, I know precisely how King John felt about barons," Arabella remarked lightly, causing Baransky to laugh, and to think she was a most sophisticated sort of female.

But when she set him down by the gate, retrieving her sister-in-law from Princess Lieven, Arabella's newly acquired veneer of worldliness was very thin indeed. Pleading a headache, she dropped off her sister-in-law on

Upper Mount Street and proceeded homeward feeling dismal.

Not even the almost supernatural instincts of Fishbank, who sent up to her room a soothing cordial, had much effect in assuaging her fit of the blue dismals. Arabella threw herself across the bed and sobbed into her pillow for reasons even she did not fully understand.

Self-pity was not a great part of her character, however, and her spirits were sufficiently restored by the time Eliza came in to dress her for dinner and a musical evening at Lady Omberseley's.

As she came floating down the stairs in a gown of sea-green spider gauze, fastening a bracelet on her wrist, she met her husband coming up, still in his riding dress.

"Ah, good day, wife," he said, amiably enough, "or should I say good evening. You are much in looks tonight."

"Thank you," Arabella said, a bit surprised. She had not expected to encounter him, and a very pretty flush filled her cheeks, barely visible in the low light of the candle sconces that framed the heavy Italian landscapes on the walls. "Where do you come from?" she asked casually, wondering if he had been with Lady Sibley.

Beast, loosening the spotted kerchief about his neck, pushed his hat beneath his arm and shrugged. "Out of the Four-in-Hands, all day. Then, tonight, I thought we might have dinner together and you would play a little music, but I see that you are otherwise engaged."

"It is only a dinner at Lady Omberseley's; you were invited also, you recall, and said that you did not care for Lady Omberseley, but as she was fashionable, I should accept," Arabella replied. "If you like, I could plead a sick headache, and we could stay at home, just the two of us—"

Beast shook his head. "Oh, no, I would not dream of depriving you of the pleasure of your friends," he said quickly. "I think, instead, I shall change, and have a look-in at Waitier's and Bond Street. Freddie Morgan is in town. Old friend of mine, you know. Probably be out quite late."

Arabella wanted to say that it was no trouble at all, and that she would far rather spend the evening at home, but instinctively comprehended that should she do so, she would betray an unbecoming interest in her contractual spouse that would certainly put him off. Instead she smiled a little unsteadily, and nodded, the plumes in her headdress waving slightly. "Just as you wish, husband," she said, and proceeded down the stairs. Fishbank was at the door to let her out into the open air, where her carriage awaited her.

She did not see Beast, his face in shadow, pause at the top of the stairs and watch her move out the door, an expression that might have been wistfulness in his eye.

Chapter
Ten

THE LONG-AWAITED AND MUCH wagered-upon boxing match was held on a watery day in a farmer's field, somewhere outside of Greenwich, an easy drive from the metropolis but far enough from the eyes of both the law and the womenfolk to enable most of the spectators to make a day of it.

Every inn and tavern for miles around had been solidly booked, and several hours before Bob Barstow was to meet Henry "The Black" Mills, the field was thronged with horses and carriages, and every other vehicle known in England—from dog carts to high-perch phaetons—as men from all walks and stations in life mingled in high anticipation of the event to come. In masculine circles, little else had been spoken of for days; if Bonaparte had chosen to escape his island exile or the Regent had staged a palace revolt in the nude, it would have been a matter of little concern, at least until it was seen which combatant could successfully trounce the other in a ceaseless number of rounds.

Bare-knuckle fighting, introduced to the gentry by the exploits of Gentleman Jackson, who ran a successful gymnasium devoted to the sport for the upper classes, had long been popular at country fairs and city arenas where there were cockfights and bullbaits. Only in the past twenty years had it become an acknowledged mania, and while Arabella and other ladies might deplore the idea of two grown men climbing into an enclosure to pummel at each other until one was rendered unconscious, all for a prize of money, it was apparently a passion among males, for it would have been hard to find a man who could not shirk his duties for the day to be there.

Sailors and soldiers, apprentices and tradesmen, beggars and nabobs, lords and layabouts were all congregating in the field, until they might have reached some thousand heads altogether, gathered in the greatest spirit of harmony and anticipation of the event to come.

Great sums of money were freely wagered, and touts wandered through the crowd offering various odds, as if they were at the racetrack. In spite of the gray skies and the damp, chilly weather, there was a holiday spirit to the gathering, and pickpockets and buskers sought to pick up some coins, each in his own way.

An hour or so earlier, a caravan of vendors had arrived from the city, and were even now offering their wares to the hungry or thirsty. Ale and small beer were freely available to a man with sixpence in his pocket, and the enticing scent of frying pastries and mutton pies rendered the air delicious. Chestnuts roasted on grills, and elegant valets spread linen cloths on the ground, for their masters to dine off hock and cold pheasant beside their carriages.

Jugglers and acrobats kept the ever-increasing crowd entertained with their antics, and women who were no more respectable than they had to be strolled among the men, blatantly offering their own wares and specialties for sale in the row of tents erected for the purpose by their fancy-men along the hedgerows that bordered the field.

Some of the men were already drunk, having arrived in that condition; others were on their way to being so, given enough trips to the ale vendors or enough sips from their own kegs. A marine and a soldier were offering each other that which, in a little while, the two pugilists in the ring would be performing professionally. The soldier was offering to draw the marine's cork, while the marine threatened his opponent with a taste of his own home brew, much to the amusement and encouragement of their fellows.

Beast Blackwater, happening upon this mise-en-scène, elegantly skirted the skirmish, as befitted a gentleman with no wish to become a combatant.

Sporty in his open-throated shirt and Belcher kerchief, wearing a blue nankeen jacket and a pair of glossily polished Hessians, with a low-crowned brown beaver firmly on his dark head, he still gave off the aura of someone who was not to be played with, and the brawlers parted around him instinctively, realising they would prefer not to have a go with him.

Beast was enjoying the sights and sounds of this day enormously, and had no idea that he exuded a sort of powerful strength that no wise man would challenge, nor was he aware of the respectful looks he received as he wended his way through the milling crowd.

His attention was focused upon the fact that somewhere in his perambulations, he had lost his brother-in-law, Rondo, as well as his manservant, the redoubtable Fishbank, and that it would be good to find at least Rondo before the actual event started. Of Fishbank's ability to sustain himself in any situation, he had but little doubt. Of Rondo's ability to be easily distracted by jugglers or ale vendors or even cyprians, he did have some experience, and his sharp, black eyes swept the crowd in search of that elusive figure.

Unlike a great many gentlemen in the viscount's station, Beast had no great dislike or even fear of mingling with the hoi polloi. He did not greatly enjoy the company of his fellow man, but that prejudice was of a general nature rather than a snobbish one. A solitary individual, Beast's preference was for his own company above that of other human beings, unless, like him, they knew how to keep to themselves, and how to comport themselves in any situation.

Nonetheless, his sojourn in America had inured him to the great cominglings of crowds, and it was as much for his own amusement as for a desire to place a goodly sum upon The Black's triumph that he had descended from the comparative safety of his own phaeton to take a stroll about. Although he probably would have preferred torture to admission, there was still within him a small boy who loved fairings and excitement such as was provided by a gathering such as this.

Two or three times he was hailed by gentlemen of his acquaintance, inviting him to sit on their carriage boxes or partake of whatever entertainments they had brought with them from town, but he only smiled and shook his head, continuing on with his stroll.

The boxing ring, little more than a canvas platform fenced in with rope, as much to keep the spectators out as the contestants in, was now in the final stages of erection by several burly workmen. The timekeepers, judges and other officials, in their very best clothing, had gathered beside the spot and were discussing, in low and important voices, the rules and regulations of the match to come.

On a high bank some five hundred yards away, Beast knew that a nuncheon repast was being laid out for himself and Rondo; the wine was uncorked and breathing, cold chicken and pheasant were laid out on a white linen cloth beside the carriage, and a mayonnaise was even now being prepared by Rondo's excellent valet, awaiting their return. There would be dark bread and strong cheese, too, and probably hothouse strawberries from the estate, served with clotted cream. Suddenly he felt hungry, his appetite stirred, and, not without some relief, he spotted his brother-in-law ahead of him, talking to someone in a closed landau.

Beast quickened his pace.

Rondo Blackwater-Younge was the very picture of a man who loves life, and one of those rare beings of whom it might be said, with some justification, that life loved him in return. Of the medium height, he had lost a great deal of his hair, so that his forehead seemed to have crawled back to the crown of his head, and his features were round and rather infant-like. Rondo was blessed with an habitual expression of such good nature that he always appeared to be smiling, even when his mood was stormy or glum. Happily, such situations were almost alien to his nature, for his was, unlike that of his wife's side of the family, a sanguine and optimistic temperament. Universally hailed as a fine fellow, he could count many friends among his acquaintance and very few enemies, and it was an adventure to stroll the length of a thoroughfare with him, be it the High in his home village or Bond Street in London, for he was sure to be universally accosted for a moment or two of pleasantries and gossip by nearly everyone he passed. Rondo's acquaintance was vast, without any sort of distinction of occupation, class or gender, and even very small children had been known to detach themselves from their nurses or their mothers, attracted to him as a moth to a flame.

Standing beside the enclosed landau, he seemed to be gazing up at some person or persons within. As he reached for his snuffbox, concealed in an inner pocket of his coat of bath superfine, his expression was that of someone who sees, hears and speaks no evil, but is always glad of the opportunity to be tempted. He dipped and took his snuff off his wrist, had a most gratifying sneeze, all the while appearing to listen to the occupant of the landau with the greatest of interest. Only Beast and others of his most intimate circle recognised the gesture as one of utter boredom, for it is unfortunate that men like Mr. Blackwater-Younge seem to attract a great many bores, perhaps as a consequence of their universal desire to please.

Beast, catching his brother-in-law's eye, read the signals conveyed in the lift of an eyebrow, but did not quicken his pace to come to his relative's rescue. Rather, as he caught sight of the crest on the landau's door, he frowned very deeply indeed, so severely that it might have been called a scowl, for he recognised that crest as belonging to the house of Sibley.

As little as he wished to speak to the man he had (along with half the male population of London, should the truth be told) cuckolded, he had even less reason to allow poor Rondo to be trapped in the ceaseless and pointless roundaboutation that comprised a conversation with the dim-witted Lord Sibley, and it was with a long-suffering sigh that he drew up beside the landau.

"There you are, Beast," Rondo said affably, "just talkin' about you. Said you might be in these parts somewhere, but had been separated by the crowd."

"Ah, yes, there you are." It was not Sibley, but Lady Sibley who leaned out of the landau, her slanted eyes looking at him with fire and ice in their depths.

Beast's eyebrow raised only a fraction of an inch as he made a curt bow. "Good day, ma'am, I trust I find you well?"

Her laughter was slightly strained as she leaned out from beneath the hood. Her breasts, magnificant as they were, spilled out of her low-cut gown. "What you mean, my dear Beast," she purred, lightly tapping his cheek with her fan, "is that you are surprised to see me here. Rondo certainly was."

Beast wondered what he had ever seen in her, aside from the convenience of her sexuality. Above all things he disliked being touched, let alone given a "playful" slap in public by a slut masquerading as a lady.

"Certainly this is no place one expects to see a lady," he said evenly.

Lady Sibley tilted her head, framed by a leghorn hat, to one side. It was the pose Reynolds had painted to make her famous, but it somehow did not work in reality. Perhaps it was the dangerous look that seeped into her eyes, behind her smile.

"I think," Rondo said carefully, replacing his hat on his head, "that I shall meander back to the phaeton and have a bite to eat. The mill is to start at noon, and it is almost that time now. Will you come with me, Beast?"

"I shall join you in a moment," Lord Blackwater said. "I have a few things to say to Lady Sibley in private, if you do not mind."

"Of course, of course, old fellow. Lady Sibley, your

servant." Rondo wisely backed away before turning tail and almost running up the hill through the crowd.

Beast, however, was not to be deferred. Negligently, and with a terrible false smile upon his face, should anyone care to glance in their direction, he leaned against the landau, propping one booted foot on the spokes of the wheel.

Lady Sibley perhaps sensed that she had finally gone too far, but, to her credit, she did not back down. Rather, she ran a pink tongue about her lips and looked down at him through her lashes.

"You must miss me by now," she said.

"You would hardly seem to need my company. You are surrounded by men," Beast replied. "Good God, Caroline! Not even Barbara would have dared to pull such a stunt, and her ton was impeccable! What can you mean, appearing at a boxing mill, and without even Sibley to lend you countenance?"

"Perhaps I have developed a passion for the sight of handsome men, stripped to the waist, pummeling each other. I have never shied away from the sight of blood, Beast. You know that."

Her long, tapered fingers drummed idly on the side of the door.

He shook his head. "Caroline, it is all over between us. I told you so when I presented that damned barege dress to you together with your congé. Certainly you should be looking forward to a newer, fresher conquest by now. You knew from the start that it was only a chance thing between us. I told you so, at the onset."

Her lips settled into a thin, hard line. "No one tells *me* when it is over," she said. "No one. *I tell them.* Do you understand, Beast? I tell them, they do not tell me. Is it that milk-and-water miss you married? Certainly the honeymoon should be over by now! One hears she dances the night away at Almack's with that handsome Russian count, no?"

Beast's look was such that she drew slightly back, breasts heaving, knowing that she had gone too far at last.

"What my wife chooses and does not choose to do cannot be any of your business," he said shortly.

Her fan snapped open, and she waved it at herself as if to calm the flush that spread across her cheeks. It was not a blush of modesty, but the chagrin of fury. Whatever modesty she had had long since departed in the train of her raucous life.

"I only tell you for your own good," she managed to say, making a quick recovery. "If your friends will not tell you the truth, then you must hear it from your enemies."

"And you, I assume, spend every Tuesday night at Almack's? Come now, the patronesses of that most respectable of establishments would as soon submit to the tortures of the martyrs as to allow you to even peer into the windows, Caroline! Come now, do not try your tricks on me, woman! It was your tricks and your avarice that made me cool on you in the first place! It was not my handsome person that bought your favours, but a diamond necklace, and a barege dress, and a handsome hunter to parade yourself in the park—and you all the while married to one of the richest men in England! You don't care for me—you never did. It was all a fig, and so you will see when you allow your wounded vanity to calm down!"

"Ah, but I have my means of gathering information. I may not be invited to the houses of the high sticklers, but that doesn't mean their husbands don't come courting me, Beast Blackwater, and so you shall find out, when you see who my latest interest is."

"I was about to say Rondo, but I realise he is too small a fish for a wide net such as yours. Anyway I have no interest in your servants' gossip, Caroline, any more than I have in you. If I retained the least interest in you, your odious conduct at the opera put a period to that!"

"I was jealous," she purred. "Jealous of another woman in your arms. You and I are very good together, you know. Very good indeed."

Beast made a formal, ironic bow. "What you mean to say is that we *were* very good together, ma'am. And now, if you will pardon me, I shall bid you not farewell, madam, but adieu. I'short, having given you your congé once, I see no reason to repeat the scene!"

With that he turned on his heel and was gone, leaving her astonished, her mouth agape, her bosom heaving within her bodice.

"Damn you, Beast Blackwater," she hissed. "Damn you!"

There was nothing in Beast's expression to indicate the rage and pain he was feeling as he casually strolled through the crowd and up the grassy knoll to the place where his phaeton was placed among the other vehicles of the gentry.

Rondo, reclining on a blanket on the grass, sipping a glass of perfect hock and sampling a morsel of cold pheasant, regarded him for storm signals, and much to his relief, saw none. Beast cast his hat into the hands of the redoubtable Fishbank and allowed his brother-in-law's valet to hand him a glass of wine.

"Bit of a turn-up, old boy?" Rondo inquired mildly.

"The lady seemed to be in some confusion as to the right state of affairs," Beast replied, draining off his wine and holding out his glass to the valet, who refilled it.

At that moment the bell rang, and the fighters entered the ring.

"Thirty quid on The Black!" Rondo exclaimed.

"Done and done again!"

Absorbed in the match, Rondo did not see the dark

look that settled upon Beast's rugged features, nor the way in which he downed his second glass of wine.

Although he would have died rather than admit to it, Lady Sibley's vicious piece of gossip concerning Arabella and the handsome Russian count had hit home. Logic told him that such a tendre as she had described was not at all in Arabella's style.

His wife, he reflected grimly, knew the rules as well as he did. They were of the same class of people, after all. It was only after the birth of the male heir that the wife could develop an outside interest. Once the succession had been assured, both parties were equally free to pursue their own interests in a marriage of convenience.

Caroline Sibley was a spiteful and jealous female, possessive and vindictive. When he had first become entangled with her, he had assumed that she knew the game as well as he did. God knew, she had played it on poor Sibley often enough. The pleasures had been physical only, and had ended when she had stormed and sulked over a diamond necklace that Sibley well could have afforded to give her, had she but strolled into Rundel and Bridge and airily asked that the bill be sent to her husband. Fat, foolish Sibley would hardly have protested any expenditure his beautiful wife wished to make. Poor sod, Beast reflected, he lived under the cat's paw. But for Beast to buy her the necklace, that frippery, overpriced string of diamonds, that had been her goal—proof of her power over him. It had been her greed that had turned him away from their liaison. Not, he hoped, that he was a cheese-paring sort of man. He had never begrudged a female anything she wanted from him, and Lord knew Barbara had run through money barefooted . . . it was simply the way in which Lady Sibley had contrived the matter, as if to flaunt her possession of him all over London, and her knowing damn and well that he was on short string until that business of his father's will could be resolved. Not that she cared—oh, no. Caroline Sibley had never cared for anything save herself. No harlot with a heart of gold. Then why had he entangled himself with such a one?

The answer, he knew, was simple. In her own vulgar and grasping way, she had somehow reminded him of Barbara. But Barbara never would have been so vicious, nor acted so badly at the end of the affair. Here he had to smile to himself, recalling just how badly the end of the affair had come about. It was impossible, he knew, to reason with a man driven half mad with lust, and he had been made so by Caroline Sibley, if only because she had reminded him of Barbara, his lost Barbara. Both of them were vixens, blond and blue-eyed vixens who would do anything to get what they wanted. But there, he understood, the resemblance ended. Whatever Barbara's sins had been, and may she rest in peace in her grave somewhere in Italy, she had been neither stupid nor greedy for material things. Her crimes had been crimes of the heart, passions acted upon that had been better left to cool. She may have crowned him with a pair of cuckold's horns, but she had never bilked him of his last few pounds and then come back asking for a five-hundred-pound silk barege dress, without so much as a wink of the eye. No, whatever Barbara's sins, she had had *bottom*. Courage, spirit, character. Lady Sibley had none of these things, and only the most passing resemblance to the late love of his life.

Still and all, he reflected, watching the fisticuffs through narrowed eyes, a tiny muscle in the side of his jaw flexing, Caroline Sibley had done him an enormous favor. She had released him from the spell of Barbara forever, and she had brought him to Arabella.

To Arabella? What was he thinking of? The second

wife he had won in a game of chance with her wastrel father? In a way, Caroline Sibley had even led him into that. Had he not been out a breathtaking sum of money for that foolish necklace, and been quietly and ever so tactfully dunned by Rundel and Bridge, he never would have married Arabella. Or indeed, have even crossed her path. And yes, on some level he was grateful for that. She had made his life comfortable for him. Not by the least word or deed that she indicated to him how awkward it must have been for her to come into his house as a stranger. Instead she had quietly and efficiently set about turning the neglected mortuary into a clean and pleasant home for him. After so many years of wandering, how pleasant it was, he realised, to come home to find a quiet and well-run household where his hat and coat were taken from him at the door, and brandy and his favourite cigarillos awaited him in his study, where his favourite meals were always on the table . . .

And if of late his wife had not been home one night out of two, he could at least content himself with the thought that he had tried, in his own way, to provide her with the recompense she deserved.

Although he was no great lover of society, he was glad enough to see her accepted so wholeheartedly into its rather spare bosom, if that was what pleased her. If he sometimes felt a little neglected in the general stir, or lost for her company, he had only to remind himself that expecting her to play Beatrice to his Benedict was not a part of their arrangement.

He had plenty of things with which to occupy himself; there were his horses and his clubs and his friends and his affairs on the estate and in business. A fortune, after all, did not manage itself, but needed, like a field of wheat, to be tended to and taken care of, and the management of his finances were not something he felt, as his father had, should be left solely to his solicitors and his man of business, any more than the overseeing of the estate should be left to a bailiff.

Soon, he thought, he would take Arabella to Blackwater—as soon as the season was over. City-bred as she was, he knew she would find much to wonder about and much that was new and different in the country. And the estate needed its lady, too. There were many places where a woman's touch was good and necessary. Arabella, he thought, was the sort of woman one could depend upon to get to know the tenants and perhaps inspire their liking as well as their respect. He knew his people respected him, but he also knew they could never like him, not in the way people liked Arabella with her common sense and her frank, open manner. Too, he rather enjoyed the vision of her at harvest time, with hay in her hair and a pitcher of small beer in her hand, pouring it out for the thirsty threshers. And in time, perhaps there would be children, Beast mused . . .

At the thought of children, the faint, unconscious smile that had been slowly appearing on his rough countenance disappeared, replaced by a frown as a prickle of jealousy penetrated his consciousness.

Damn the woman, he thought. It was just an innocent friendship. Baransky was hardly the sort of fellow Arabella would pick out as her *lover*.

Was he?

No, no, of course not, he reassured himself. Such a frippery fellow, and something of a countercoxcomb, too, if Blackwater did not miss his guess. Wrote poetry! No real man wrote poetry, did he?

Well, there was that Byron fellow, and look what merry hell he played among the ladies . . .

Not Arabella. Hadn't he, Beast, shown her every marital attention? No need for her to cast an eye about.

Valiantly he tried to suppress the twinges of a naturally jealous nature, and instead concentrate on the fight, now going into the eleventh round.

Both boxers were bloody, and The Black was heaving slightly, as if winded, but still full of go.

But one thing was for sure, Beast thought darkly. Having once suffered the humiliation of being crowned with a cuckold's horns, he would never, ever repeat the experience. Unlike the half-witted Lord Sibley, he knew how to deal with such situations.

The match went into twenty rounds, and ultimately it was The Black who was paraded, triumphant, through the throng of lustily cheering men.

"What a great go!" Rondo exclaimed, his face flushed with excitement. "Was there ever such a man, or such a match? Gentleman Jackson must be rightly proud of his protégé!"

"And well he should be, too!" Beast exclaimed. "What a roundhoue punch that last one was! But he managed to sink it in, right under Barstow's left jab!"

Both of them had had more than a little to drink, and their faces glowed as much with the effect of the wine as with the excitement of the match.

It only seemed, in the proper mood of things, the thing to do to stop in at the first tavern they spied on the London Road, already filled to bursting with other patrons of the fancy celebrating their victory or consoling their losses at the match they had just attended.

Men of all classes and stations stood four deep at the bar, laughing and shouting at one another and calling for more ale, more beer, until the perspiring landlord and his minions were hard pressed to keep up with the demand.

All the private rooms had been spoken for, much to Rondo's dismay, but Beast, of a more democratic spirit, elbowed and joked his way into the center of the tap, where he towered over nearly every one of his fellow patrons in his low-crowned brown beaver, seeking the attention of the tapster with a wave of his hand, liberally loaded down with coins.

He had just shouted his order over the din to the harassed boy pulling the taps when he felt a tug at his shoulder and looked down to see the florid face of his father-in-law.

Sir Bosworth's countenance betrayed not just the dissipation of his life's habitude, but also a severe degree of anxiety. Beast, who had never been able to look at Sir Bosworth without experiencing a feeling of profound dislike, now found this unwanted and unexpected reunion repugnant, although he did not betray, by any show of emotion, his feelings.

"What a mill!" Sir Bosworth said, pleasantly enough, even though beads of sweat were standing out on his forehead, and the hand that dabbed a kerchief to his flesh was trembling.

All things considered Beast found this a very odd opening remark indeed, but held his peace, waiting to see what Sir Bosworth would say next. He was not disappointed.

"Trust m'daughter is doing well with you?"

When Beast did not reply, Sir Bosworth smiled a ghastly smile, showing a great many aged and yellowing teeth. Thirty years of self-indulgence and dissipation were written into the lines and the small veins on his face, as well as the scarlet network in his eyes. "I say, old man, seeing as how we're in-laws and all of that, I wonder if you might help me out. I find myself a trifle embarrassed—over-wagered, as it were. Backed the wrong man to the tune of a few hundred quid . . . came 'way without my purse . . ."

"How much do you need?" Beast asked coldly.

"Five hundred pounds would do it for now, old man," Sir Bosworth said, looking hopeful.

"And for later?" Beast asked him, one eyebrow raised slightly.

Sir Bosworth bit his lip. "Well, then," he said in a half-whining tone, "seeing as how you never made a proper settlement on Arabella, and how's we've been deprived of her company, as well as her services about the house since she left . . ."

"And seeing as how she brought no dowry with her, I should say a thousand pounds for you, my man, and no more," Beast finished coolly. "Good God, was there ever a more unnatural parent?" he finally asked, pushed beyond endurance. "Arabella has been my wife for nearly seven weeks, and not once have you or your wife as much as sent a footman about to inquire as to how she is doing! For all you knew, or cared, she might have been sold into white slavery in South America!"

"There've been reasons why I never got about to see the girl," Sir Bosworth replied in his annoying whine. "I've been sick. All this social life, it's bad for my health, you know."

"Social life!" Beast retorted. "Is that what you call it, then? Eating and drinking and whoring with Prinny until someone either passes out or passes over? Hardly salubrious occupations, sir! Although ruinous, I am certain."

"Anway, Lady Ivers says that my Arabella is all the rage now, moves in the very highest reaches of the ton! Says she wonders why the chit can't be bothered to send for her sisters to share her good fortune! Do me good to have the pack of them off my hands! Eating me out of house and home they are, and not a man in Christendom's appearing to take 'em off my hands! Chitter chitter here, chitter chitter there, and not a moment's peace does a man have in his own home. One thing you could say for Arabella, she didn't *chitter!*"

"No, she does not do that," Beast had to agree with a reluctant smile.

"Sons were what I wanted, and daughters is what I got! Damn me if I ain't cursed!" Sir Bosworth sighed. "No luck, no luck at all! I don't suppose you'd be interested in a sure thing at Newmarket?"

"Absolutely not!" Beast replied fervently. From an inner pocket, he withdrew his card and scribbled a few words on the back with a gold pencil, handing it to Sir Bosworth. "Here! Take this to my man of business in the City, and he will give you a thousand pounds!"

Sir Bosworth almost collapsed inward with relief, so grateful was he to be out of what he termed the River Tick. "I'll repay you! I'll repay you!" he promised. "I'm telling you, this sure thing at Newmarket will come in at a hundred to one, and then—"

"You my repay me by coming around to see your daughter one morning. If you cannot fulfill the form of a father, the very least you may do is pay attention to the conventions! Not for anything in this world would I have Arabella appear in any way to be slighted by her family, whatever my opinion may be of them!"

"Of course, of course," Sir Bosworth promised freely, secreting the card in his pocket book and tucking it away in a safe place within his coat. "Of course, dear boy, be only too happy to see the dear girl! Bring m'wife and her sisters, too, if you like!"

"That," Beast said firmly, "Would be doing it *too* brown! You alone will suffice!"

Turning to claim his tankards of ale, he did not see Sir Bosworth Ivers practically skip away into one of the bespoken private parlours.

Seated by the open window, pressed by a coterie of somewhat dubious suitors, Lady Sibley looked up at him.

"I trust you are no longer embarrassed," she said sharply, holding out her hand, palm up and waggling her fingers. "Come, pay your debt! Your vows are no good to me!"

If it was possible, Sir Bosworth flushed a deeper red than before. Lady Sibley's friends were a crowd that even he found fast going—a set of Greeks, Captain Sharps and other hangers-on in the gaming hells of the metropolis. It is one thing to make a wager with a young and pretty woman in the privacy of her landau, after one has had one or two (or three or four) glasses of Madeira, and quite another to have that female turn upon you in the most predatory fashion when it comes time to claim her debt.

"I, er, don't have the cash," he said. "But I did manage to procure a voucher from my son-in-law, who I happened to encounter in the taproom."

"What! Beast here! How amusing!" Lady Sibley said, a bit shrilly. She was still stinging from the set-down he had delivered her that afternoon.

"Yes, yes, daresay he's gone on about his business now. The place was crowded and—"

"Beast gave you his vow?" Caroline Sibley almost purred. "But of course. You are his father-in-law, are you not? Very considerate indeed, and I am certain his rate of interest was far lower than mine would have been, had I been forced to carry you."

"I shall have the money for you the first thing tomorrow morning," Sir Bosworth promised.

But Lady Sibley was looking at him in a most peculiar way. Her demeanour, which had been cold before, suddenly became quite warm, and she smiled, dismissing a gentleman in a bottle-green waistcoat and offering Sir Bosworth his place beside her on the settle.

"You know, I really would like to hear how Beast and your daughter first met," she said, tilting her head to one side and allowing the bodice of her gown to slide down just a little bit lower. "It is such an amusing story, that, you know." With the tip of her fan, she touched the hairy corner of Sir Bosworth's earlobe. "Won't you tell me about it just one more time?"

Sir Bosworth had never been one to stop when he sensed trouble. Flattered by her attentions and more than a little distracted by the way in which she was devoting all of her attention to him, he coughed. For the life of him, he could not recall ever having told her the story of Arabella's marriage before, but perhaps he had.

She was pouring another glass of wine and putting it into his hand. "Now," she purred, "Do, please, tell me *all* about it."

Chapter
Eleven

"PAPA? YOU SAW PAPA?"

The breakfast room was the most cheerful chamber in Blackwater House. Hoping to take advantage of the southern exposure, Arabella had caused it to be done in shades of butter and cream, to make it feel, even on a day like today, when the city was smothered beneath a blanket of thick, wet fog, as if it were bright and sunny outside. A cheerful fire burned in the coal grate and the remains of a hearty breakfast lay on the sideboard, waiting to be cleared. Kidneys, kippers, bacon and scrambled eggs had long since grown cold, and of the toast on the rack on the table between them, there was no need to speak; it had turned frigid and stiff as a board. Only the teapot on its silver stand remained at the ready, the little flame beneath causing it to send up tiny puffs of steam from time to time, like a child's breath on a frosty morning.

At his end of the table, Beast Blackwater, in a highly embroidered dressing gown of Chinese dragons and swirling sunflowers, peered over the top of the *Morning Post* at his wife, temporarily at a loss for a reply.

He had not expected such a casual remark to be greeted with such consternation, and he raised his eyebrow slightly as he regarded her. Her next question surprised him even more.

"How much did he touch you for?" she asked in a rather weary tone of voice, turning her Limoges teacup around and around in her hands, two bright spots of colour appearing in her cheeks as they always did when she was surprised or upset, he had deducted in the brief course of their marriage.

He shrugged. "Only a thousand pounds," he said lightly.

Arabella looked up at him. The teacup rang clearly as she replaced it in the saucer and took up a slice of cold toast from the rack, which she absently began to butter. "A thousand pounds! Oh, husband, I wish you had not. Now he will see you as a sure touch!"

"Hard words," Beast replied, rattling the pages of his newspaper, somewhat discomfited by this unexpected reaction to his generosity with her father, after all.

Arabella, he noticed, now that she had his attention and the *Post* did not, was looking particularly pretty this morning. She wore an ivory muslin morning dress, worked into many small pleats and trimmed with lace and rose ribbons. He noted that she had taken to wearing a cap, this one of lawn and lace, tied rather dashingly beneath one ear, and he sought to distract her from her agitation by remarking how fetching she looked.

But as pleased as she was by his flattering notice of

her, Arabella was not to be distracted by compliments on her caps, which, after all, only represented her status as a married lady, and brought her around again to the subject of Papa.

With short, agitated strokes, she buttered the toast she had no intention of eating. "Forgive me, husband, I know it is not my place to tell you what you can and cannot do with your funds—but you must understand! Giving money to Papa to settle his gaming debts is like pouring oil on a flame! He will only take the money and place it on another sure thing, and lose that, too! His gambling is a sort of mania with him, a sickness. Just as some people cannot stop drinking gin or taking opium, so he cannot stop gaming! We were only fortunate that my grandfather tied things up in such a way that Papa cannot touch his principal—only the income, or he would have gambled the very roof over our heads away, if he could have!"

She tried to keep her tone matter-of-fact, but her husband was not so self-absorbed that morning that he could not read the very real anxiety beneath her words.

She tried to smile and the toast crumbled away, brittle and dry, beneath her hands. "Do I sound like an unnatural daughter?" she asked, and without waiting for his reply, continued onward. "But *you* must know that my father is hardly a natural parent—only consider the circumstances of our marriage! Please, I beg of you, don't allow my father to think of you as a source of funding for his—his *obsessions*! It is not good for him!"

Stung, Beast straightened his spine, feeling very much as if his good deed had won him only a disapproving scold from his wife. His brow darkened.

Sensing his mood, Arabella put out her hand. "I know that you are trying to do what is right, Beast, and you have been so very good to me—" Arabella dropped her eyes, lest he read the truth in them and turn away from her. She bit her lower lip. "Well, you must see that Papa is profligate, and that once he believes you will bail him out of the River Tick, you will have no peace!"

Slightly mollified, Beast leaned back in his chair. He wanted to tell her he would do anything for her, but he contented himself with a commonplace. "I must, of course, trust you in these matters. Sir Bosworth is, after all, your father, but I should very much dislike to hear it said that I did not relieve him of his distress when I married his daughter, you know."

"No one who knew Papa—or knew you—would say such a thing!" Arabella cried loyally.

"He did say that he would call upon you," Beast added, editing out his own part in those proceedings.

"Papa would say *anything*, do anything where gambling is concerned. Anyway, I doubt very much that he will. He has never been one to face the consequences of— of his own folly." Even, she thought, when his folly has brought me you, but she dared not say so aloud. "And of course, I doubt very much that my stepmother would allow it. You saw *her* reaction to my leaving Half Moon Street. I am certain that she is glad enough to have washed her hands of such a wretched stepdaughter as I am!"

Beast shrugged. "Whatever. I only meant it to be a gesture of kindness."

"Would a noggin of gin be a kindness to a drunkard?" Arabella asked.

Nettled, Beast shook his head. He hated for anyone to point out his transgressions, even when they were glaringly obvious. That Arabella, normally the least critical and most accommodating of wives, should do so came as a bit of a surprise to him, and he said, a bit petulantly, "No, I suppose not. But, Arabella, you know the estrangement between you and your family *will* cause talk, taken as it is, with the circumstances of our marriage."

132

Arabella failed to detect the storm warnings in her husband's tone of voice, perhaps because she was seeking to control her own feelings. "People will always talk, no matter what," she said flatly. "Let them conjecture as they will. But surely, all the world must know that Sir Bosworth Ivers's haunts are those of the Regent—Brighton and Carleton House, rather than Almack's and Princess Lieven's, and those worlds hardly connect." Her tone was dry and her smile was thin.

With rare insight into the feelings of another, it suddenly dawned upon Beast Blackwater that his wife was not overly anxious to have any further dealings with her family. Having witnessed their behaviour firsthand, he could readily sympathise, and with more empathy than he had ever felt for another person before, he could not find it in his heart to blame her for her feelings. As she had said, it was unlikely that Sir Bosworth would put in an appearance at Blackwater House, and therefore he felt very little compunction to tell her he had invited his unhappy father-in-law to do so.

Although anxious for Arabella's sake to maintain proper appearances, Beast had as little desire to be continually pulling his father-in-law out of the River Tick as he had to inform his wife that he had, albeit with the best will in the world, unthinkingly invited her estranged parent to call upon his daughter. It was with an unaccustomed sense of guilt that he rattled his newspaper and cleared his throat, resenting her only a little for drawing his attention to his mistakes. This was a new experience for him, and not entirely a pleasant one, especially since he was quite used to Arabella being totally uncritical of his actions.

"Husband, I suppose this may not be a very good time to broach this subject," Arabella said, after a few moments, "but it seems to me that it really *must* be discussed."

"Have you dropped a fortune at silver loo or bought a dress for a thousand guineas?" he asked casually, trying to make amends for his former behaviour with a bantering tone.

Arabella had picked up her embroidery, and her needle darted in and out of the heavy cloth, picking up the ghostly image of what appeared to be a bouquet of flowers. She frowned as she worked, not meeting his eyes.

"No, nothing like that," she said at last. "It is only that since the end of the Season is coming upon us, I thought that perhaps we should have some sort of entertainment, to repay everyone for their kindness in entertaining us."

"What sort of entertainment did you have in mind?" Beast asked cautiously.

In and out the needle darted, defining the petal of a moss rose in long-and-short stitch. Arabella looked at him from beneath her lashes. "Well, Charlotte will be out of black gloves very soon, you know, and she thought that perhaps we ought to give a ball—or something." The stitches wavered slightly, neither so long nor so short as they had been before. "I said, of course, that seemed to me to be rather more than we might be able to manage right now, especially since you are not at all fond of that sort of thing, and that perhaps a dinner might be better—"

Beast sighed, but not as inwardly as he thought he had. "If Charlotte says there must be a ball, then I suppose there must be. In matters of social form, you know that I must always yield to Charlotte, and to *your* desires, wife. Of course you must entertain here! I have quite forgotten the form. When were you thinking of holding this ball?"

"Well," Arabella said cautiously, "it need not be a ball, you know. In fact, Charlotte said that were her house larger, she and Rondo would of course be holding one in our honour, but since they have always used the ballroom at Blackwater House to bring out their daughters and whatnot, but it need only be a few couples, if you like, and some champagne and some dancing and a card room. Just to repay all the invitations, you see."

"Yes, we have been invited everywhere, of late," Beast admitted, without much relish. "Well, do as you like. I suppose I need not do anything but make an appearance at the proper time in black tie?"

In spite of herself Arabella smiled at her husband, who could, sometimes, behave remarkably like a small boy when the matters of society were pressed with him. "Oh, no, really, husband, if you think it would be odious or dull, we need not—after all, it is the end of the Season, and we may do it next year just as well, when more people are in town and things are—"

Beast waved his hand in the air. "No, no, let us do it now," he said. "Get it over with. Of course, you must have things just as you like. After all, you are Lady Blackwater now and I cannot gainsay you anything you would reasonably like to do—"

It was meant as a kind gesture, of course, but Arabella interpreted it to remind her that he felt himself under obligation to her from the circumstances of their marriage.

She flushed and looked down at the embroidery in her lap. "Just as you would wish," she answered, and wondered what she meant by that.

But it seemed to sail over Beast's dark, curly head. He regarded her with his dark eyes, a faint curl of amusement on his lips. If she had declared that she wished to reunite all the major players of the Congress of Vienna in the drawing room, he would not have refused her, but prudence kept him from saying this aloud. Why should he discomfit her? How very pretty she looked, he thought, with her lace mobcap and morning dress, and her embroidery. He had noted that her hands were never idle.

When she was not reading or playing the pianoforte, she was working on what she hoped, she said, would become chair covers for the family dining room.

He remained amazed that she could coax flowers and forms from her skeins of wool. But then, before her marriage, he reflected, she had had much time alone in which to hone her embroidery. Doubtless that unhappy house on Half Moon Street had every remaining piece of furniture covered with her craftwork.

For some odd reason, his voice was choked when he spoke again. "Of course, you know, you can leave it all to the admirable Fishbank. He can do just as you wish, deal with the caterers and all of that. I suppose you will want a pink silk tent and dinner for twenty or thirty couples? All that sort of thing? It has been so long since there was a ball here—" He thought about Barbara and broke off. She was *not* a subject that would ever be open for discussion with him, not even with her successor. Not for the first time, he found himself wondering if he would have had the sense to recognise Arabella's charms over those of Barbara in his salad days. When he thought about his erstwhile preference for females like Caroline Sibley, he could only shudder. But of course, it was out of the question to confide these thoughts to his lady-wife. Doubtless she would have been horrified if she had known that her husband had done something so thoroughly unfashionable as to fall in love with his own spouse.

To distract himself he picked up some letters lying beside his plate and slid them open with his table knife. "When were you thinking of holding this durbar?" he asked again, before scanning the crabbed and somewhat awkward hand he recognised as belonging to his bailiff at Blackwater Manor.

"The end of the month—if that would suit you, of course," Arabella suggested, a little timidly. She was torn between her very natural desire to repay the hospitality of her new friends and the more important desire to please her husband. After the discussion they had had this morning concerning her father, she felt quite hesitant in bringing up yet another touchy subject. Now, with a profound sense of relief that the hurdle had been mounted, she was able to enjoy a small, sanguine smile as she studied the man she had impetuously married, with his dark head bent over his letter.

He could never be anyone's idea of an Adonis, not being possessed, as was Count Baransky, of perfect beauty, but then she would not have wanted him any other way, save with his high cheekbones, his deep-set eyes and his long, tapering fingers, even now drumming on the table-cloth as he frowned, reaching into his robe for his spectacles, fitting them over his ears as he read. In her eyes, he was possessed of far more masculine beauty than Alexi Baransky could ever hope to aspire to, and she rather yearned to lean across the table and stroke his thick, bushy brows simply because they were a part of *him*. Since ladies were not supposed to have such thoughts, especially ladies poking a needle in and out of their embroidery at the breakfast table, Arabella had to bite her lip repressively.

"Lord," Beast said, quite unexpectedly. "This is terrible!"

"Trouble?" Arabella asked in concern.

"I'll say there is! Whitten, my bailiff, writes that our entire south pasture had been flooded out, and that the tide ditches need some extensive repair before the snows come in this winter. I see no choice but to go down to Blackwater immediately." He handed the letter over to Arabella. "I've been neglecting things on the estate for far too long, it's clear, and now I'm paying the price."

Arabella scanned the bailiff's anxious scrawl, but, city-bred and knowing nothing of rents, tenants and agriculture, she could make little or no sense of this communication, save that Mr. Whitten seemed quite anxious to have his lordship's presence in order to set matters to rights again, and the sooner the better.

"It sounds very desperate indeed," she said hesitantly. "Although I do not perfectly understand what he means by tide ditches and yield and rack rents."

"No, of course you wouldn't, I am forgetting," Beast said, ringing the bell to summon Fishbank. "Suffice to say that since I have been gone, a great many things have not been attended to as they should have been, which is not to say that Whitten is not a fine bailiff, which he is, but he can't be expected to continue to assume all responsibility. I have not been attending to my duty as I should, from having stayed so long away."

"Are things so very bad?" Arabella asked, concerned.

"Not so very bad yet, but I have forgotten that the Manor is where I should be. I should leave today, as a matter of fact. Can you manage without me?"

"For how long?" Arabella asked.

Beast shrugged impatiently. "However long it will take to set matters to rights again. I had hoped that after the season was over, we would go down together. After all, the tenants will want to meet you, have some sort of a ceremony, I'm sure, and Blackwater is our home. Our real home."

With the prospect of returning to the country, Beast was more alive than she had ever seen him, and she suddenly realised that his real love was the land, his land, not this life in town.

"I—I could come with you, if you like. There is certainly nothing here that I cannot live without. And I would like to see Blackwater Manor, and meet your people and your tenants. Perhaps I could even be of some help."

Beast all but laughed at her as he rose from the table in a swirl of embroidered dressing gown, placing a hand on her shoulder. "Oh, no, wife! I would not deprive you of town pleasures. That would be most unfair. I am certain that you would find yourself dead bored, buried away in the country with no one to talk to all day, and nothing to do but attend church and a few assemblies full of provincial dowds. And I would be away all day, and too tired at night to do little more than sleep by the fire in a pair of muddy boots. No, wait until the season is over, and then you may come down and be assured of a warm welcome from my people and the tenants. There is nothing you can do now. And besides, I would not deprive you of your social life!"

"Just as you like," Arabella said. For a moment, she placed her hand on top of his, resting on her shoulder.

"I trust you will be all right?" Beast asked, but he was already thinking of the country, like a dog that has smelled the game, and his thoughts were not with her.

No, she thought, not like a dog, like a schoolboy released from his classes for a sudden holiday. "Fishbank, there you are!" he cried, when that worthy entered the door. "We're off to the country! Whitten has called us down! Pack my things and we'll take the phaeton—oh, Arabella, you do not mind if I take Fishbank with me for a while, do you? I can send him back in plenty of time for the ball, if you like—"

"Oh, no," Arabella said with far more cheer than she was feeling. "You two go on—I am sure that everything will be just fine here."

Beast was draining the last of his tea out of the cup, with a snap in his eyes and a glow about him. The country was what mattered to him. Arabella could not quite understand, but she could sympathise.

"I'm sure that Russian count fella can take you

wherever you need to go," he said, gathering up his papers. "And m'sister Charlotte, she can look after you, too."

Arabella gave a little laugh she was far from feeling. "Oh, I am certain that I shall be perfectly all right. You go on ahead, and should you need anything, you have only to send for it."

"I say. Fishbank, we might be able to get in some shooting, you know," Beast was saying as he went, unthinking, to plant a hasty kiss on his wife's cheek, recollected himself, awkwardly stroked her shoulder, and strode out of the room without a backward glance.

Arabella watched him go, feeling more than a little disappointed and rather deserted as well. Slowly she sat down again, and poked her needle through her embroidery.

At least, Beast Blackwater thought as he tore up the stairs, in the country he had problems he knew how to deal with.

Chapter
Twelve

"ALORS. SO, *MON AMIE*, *M. la Bête* has left you to your own devices while he goes into the country," Alexi, Count Baransky drawled to his hostess.

He was perfectly at home in her drawing room, sprawled among the cushions on her little couch in an attitude of perpetual ennui. It was a pose that had become quite fashionable within the last fortnight among the dandy set, and the count had spent a good many hours in private, before a mirror, rehearsing it. With any luck it might remain in vogue for yet another month, and he was most anxious to demonstrate it before a trusted friend before taking it into the greater world.

Arabella, more primly seated in a chair beside the fireplace, poked her needle in and out of her linen canvas in a series of Cretan stitches filling up a geranium leaf. She was not paying as much attention to her friend's attitude as he supposed, and doubtless this was a small mercy for both of them. "Into the country," she said mournfully. "I wanted to go, but he said no. I think he was *relieved* to get away from me."

Baransky, idly sorting her embroidery wools into colours, held a strand of very pale peach up to the light and squinted at it.

"Men are always glad to get away from the women," he remarked without malice. "In my country it is even more so than here. When they are away from the ladies, they can relax and do all the things they think properly masculine, you know. It is necessary, just as it is necessary from the ladies' point of view to get away from the men."

While Arabella mulled this over, the Russian count flicked an imaginary speck of dust from his exquisitely tailored coat of blue bath superfine, the very height of Nugee's florid art. He stole a glance at himself in the pier glass over the mantelpiece, to be certain that his neckcloth suffered no disrepair of its carefully arranged folds that nearly prevented him from moving his head toward either shoulder.

"What do men do when they're away from the ladies?" Arabella asked, sipping from the Madeira at her elbow and helping herself to another macaroon from the plate on the table.

"What do the men do?" the count repeated, squinting at two differing strands in shades of rose and perceiving a subtle difference. "The men go to boxing matches and horse races, and to visit cyprians, who are of course, females, but, by the very nature of their employment, inclined to enjoy masculine pursuits—or at least to pretend that they do. Men go to their clubs, to Tattersall's, they go shooting, they hunt the stag and the boar, they smoke cigarillos, they swear and they boast, and they open their collars and put their boots up on the table and drink rather too much port, and associate with people their ladies would not approve of—"

"What! Besides the cyprians?"

"Oh, yes. You would be amazed at the associations men form that their wives would not like at all. Their grooms and their gamekeepers and their farmers and their rakish bachelor friends—all sorts of persons of whom they are certain their ladies would not approve. *Nostalgie de la boue*, you know, as Rousseau so rightly says. You see, civilisation is the occupation of the ladies, with their children and their servants and their habits of saying, 'John, please do not put your filthy boots up on the furniture,' or 'do not let those dogs track mud on my rugs,' or 'do not bring that vile, disgusting groom into the drawing room,' or whatever."

"*I* never say any of those things!" Arabella cried, much stung. "Never, ever, ever! Beast knows he is perfectly free to do as he wishes within his own home!"

"Ah, but you see, from childhood on, it is women who drill these things into the men. Believe me, I know. I had an English governess. And if I had had a Russian governess, she would doubtless have been a great deal worse, for Miss Aubrey, you see, being English, thought that certain things were quite within keeping with my sex, and was a great believer in the out-of-doors."

Arabella laughed. It was a nice sound, for she had not laughed in the several days that her husband had been gone. It was enough to make Baransky turn his head to look at her hopefully, even if it did make him disarrange his neckcloths. "That is the sort of thing you should compose your poetry about," she said, "rather than poems about the colour of someone's eyes, or some imaginary Byron-scape full of pirates and Turks."

"Perhaps," Baransky admitted, "but that would hardly be fashionable, you know, and I *must* be in fashion. If I were not, my cousin would make me go back to Russia, and things are so very dull there right now."

"Very true! The princess is a stickler for all things to be in the mode," Arabella replied, tongue firmly in cheek. "And what else do men do when they are away from the ladies? What do you do, for instance, Alexi?"

He sighed a hearty sigh full of Russian melancholia. "When I am away from you, I do not exist," he announced.

"Stuff and nonsense," Arabella replied firmly. "Although of course, I am flattered, even though I know it's not one bit true! You are by far the most odiously fashionable person I know, and you must go a hundred places without me!"

"Yes, but it is only the ones that you permit me to escort you to that have any meaning for me," Baransky said gallantly. "All the world knows, Arabella, that were you not a virtuous wife, I would be the happiest man in London."

"So you would like people to believe! You know perfectly well that as long as you can appear to be wearing the willow for me, you can avoid the snares all the matchmaking mamas in London are casting out for you."

"Very true. I do not think I should like to marry an English girl. They are not restful, and I am a man who likes his rest."

"Fudge! What you mean is they are far too independent and spirited for your Oriental temperament, Alexi. I know you! You want some cow-eyed ninny who will hang on your every word as if it were Gospel and think you the most perfect human being in existence when you don't come home for a fortnight. No Englishwoman would put up with that sort of Turkish treatment, let me assure you!"

The count shrugged. He reached for a macaroon and bit into it lazily. "Anyway, it doesn't matter. My parents have arranged a marriage for me with a Russian princess. When I go home, I shall marry her and have many children and a great deal of money. I can only hope that she is restful!"

"You mean you've never met her?"

Alexi shook his head. "No. Not since we were very small. But I am sure she will be more restful than you—and far less cruel to me!"

"Cruel! I?" Arabella asked, laughing. "Alexi, you can be a perfect beast when you want to be!"

"You spurn my passion, what else can I say?" he asked, full of his own logic. "I certainly do everything in my power to win over the beautiful Lady Blackwater, and she sits in her drawing room and laughs at me while I sort her embroidery wools."

"And a very good job you're doing of it, too. When I finish these chair covers, I shall embroider you a waist-coat—*after* I have done one for my husband, off course!"

"There! You see? Cruel!" The count shook his head, consoling himself with yet another macaroon from the plate on the table.

"Tell me what else you do when you are not with me," Arabella commanded Alexi idly, perhaps afraid that if not distracted, he might be inspired to read her some of his poetry.

"I visit my tailor, I play cards with some friends from the embassy, I stroll about and observe your city—but you must know what I do when I am not with you, for I tell you all about my days in the most exhausting detail."

"You tell me what you think I ought to know. Tell me something you do that I should not know about."

"Something I should not tell you that I do," the count repeated. "Well, once, you know, I had a little affaire with a very respectable married lady. I met her at a military review; her husband was a colonel in the Light Dragoons."

"Do I know her?" Arabella asked teasingly.

The count gave her a very repressive look. "Even if you did, I would not mention her name, since that would be very improper indeed," he said firmly.

Chastened, Arabella bit her lip to conceal her smile. "Men have such odd ideas. It was perfectly all right for you to have an affaire with this lady, but not to tell me her name!"

"Be that as it may," the count replied, very prim, for him. "Such a wonderful English expression—"

"Come on, Alexi! I die for the rest of the story!" Arabella cried.

"Well, since the colonel's lady was out of the middle class—and there is nothing quite so respectable as the English middle class, you know, anywhere! Well, we were forced to find some rather imaginative ways to meet. One night we both put on masks and dominoes and made a rendezvous at Vauxhall Gardens!"

"You did not! Say you did not!" Arabella cried, more impressed with the wickedness of actually going to the notorious place, than with the circumstances of her friend's affaire with the respectable lady. "She wouldn't! Not if she was so respectable!"

"Oh, but she did, and so did I," Alexi said complacently. "Indeed, my dear, you would be amazed at the sort of ladies and gentlemen who have been known to make a rendezvous there!"

"Names! Places! Dates!" Arabella cried. Her eyes were very wide indeed.

But the count merely laughed. "For a female who thinks herself very well up on the world, Arabella, you can be surprisingly naive sometimes," he said gently. "There are a thousand little ways to have an affaire, if one is so inclined, and to have it very discreetly, too. Vauxhall Gardens are—well, more of a sort of saturnalia."

"What happens there?"

Alexi examined his perfectly manicured nails for signs of imperfections. He frowned slightly. "Well, one pays a small fee to the gatekeeper, and there is usually an orchestra, and dancing, and little tables where one may sit and watch the dancing and drink a little wine or eat a pastry or two—but these are hardly up to the standards of your excellent chef!"

"I daresay it is not the food that entices people there. What else? Being wicked?" Arabella asked innocently.

The count selected another macaroon from the plate. "Vauxhall," he said in somewhat resigned tones. "Well, there is, you understand, a somewhat general air of licence particularly on the revelry nights, when everyone comes masked, all sorts of people from every station in life, from thieves in the Seven Dials to some very great ladies indeed. They do say that Princess Caroline used to—but there, I gossip, and I should not do that!" Alexi glanced at Arabella, who appeared eager for more details.

"There are also the gardens themselves, full of little grottoes and boxwood mazes and all sorts of secluded spots where one may be private with another person in the darkness. It is *very* fast, you see," he finished a little lamely. "The masks and dominoes and disguises . . ."

"Alexi . . ." Arabella drawled. She had set aside her embroidery, and was looking at him with a mischievous expression.

He threw up his hands as if she had offered him a blow. "Oh, no! Not me! You will have to find someone else! I refuse!" he said firmly. "Beast, he will kill me now without much hope! If he were to find out that I had taken you to Vauxhall, there would be hell to pay!"

"But he won't know! He's been in the country for a week, and the only message I have had is that he doesn't know when he'll be back, but not to plan on seeing him for at least another fortnight." She tilted her head slightly, and there was a flash of what Arabella *could* be, if she had ever been encouraged to exercise her strength of will—there was a strain of the Ivers hedonism in her blood. "Alexi, just for an hour, please? We need only go and come away again. It is something I should love to see, you know."

"It is not something for a virtuous wife," Alexi said firmly. "Suppose someone were to spot us there—*then* where would you be?"

"Oh, fudge! You just said that everyone is in dominoes and masks; who would recognise us out of so many people? Just for an hour, Alexi, and then we might go on to Almack's or some other really drearily respectable place as a matter of penance."

"It is bad *ton*," Alexi said sulkily.

"What bad ton could it be if *you* did it?" Arabella asked. "Since you set the styles, it must be all the crack!"

"Arabella, what maggot is in your head?" Alexi asked. "This is not at all like you!"

"Then perhaps it should be like me! My husband seems to prefer the company of fast women, after all," Arabella said, a little shakily.

The count dabbed at his forehead with his lawn handkerchief. "I see! It is all to make your husband jealous! I forbid it! I will not go with you!"

"Very well," Arabella said, "I shall go alone! See if I don't! I have never been so bored in my life as I have been of late, cooped up in this house all alone, while Beast is off frolicking in the country. Why, I'll just wager that he has Lady Sibley with him!"

"Now, that would be bad ton," Alexi said, hoping to divert her.

But Arabella, set upon a course, was not to be waylaid. "I'll go alone, if you won't go with me!" she said.

"I thought we were here today to talk about the arrangements for your ball," the count said with a sigh. "And now look! I am being blackmailed—yes, *blackmailed*, that is the word I want, into taking you to a haunt of vice!"

"Oh, Alexi, does that mean you will do it?" Arabella asked. She was all smiles, and quite in her best looks when pleased. "Good, kind friend! I promise I shall behave myself and not give you a moment's grief, really I won't!"

Alexi sank back into the cushions, exhausted. "Very well," he said, sighing. "But don't say I didn't warn you when your husband gets wind of this and kills me on the duelling field and has you locked into a nunnery!"

"Oh, don't be silly, people don't do those things anymore. It will be greatly amusing, you wait and see!"

"I am told that hell is greatly amusing, yet I have no desire to visit there," the count replied sulkily.

"Fudge!" Arabella replied, perfectly pleased with her first foray into wickedness. That would certainly show Beast, she thought, that she was every bit as capable of the fire and spark he seemed to admire in Lady Sibley and the late Barbara. It was a sudden decision, and yet it was based upon weeks of frustration.

"Mrs. Blackwater-Younge," the first footman announced, and that lady, in pale shades of mauve, entered the room, drawing off her gloves. "Princess Lieven!" That lady, in green, followed.

"Not a word to Charlotte or the princess!" Arabella hissed to Count Baransky, who merely rolled his eyes as he rose from his cushions to greet his cousin and Mrs. Blackwater-Younge.

"My dear child!" the princess said, standing on tiptoe to receive the kiss Baransky planted on his cousin's cheek. "Alexi, you monopolise Arabella's time most dreadfully, I fear! We do not see you at Lady Champlain's rout this morning!" She seated herself on the sofa beside her cousin and proceeded to eat the very last macaroon, much to his annoyance.

Greeting her sister-in-law and signalling to the footman for more Madeira and macaroons, Arabella managed to reply, "Since my husband is out of town, I am very dull company indeed. Alexi has been good enough to come and keep me company today. We were talking about the plans for our ball, were we not, Alexi?" She shot him a meaningful glance and he nodded, without missing a beat.

"Something other than a pink tent, I thought. One sees pink silks tents everywhere this season."

"My very thought," Mrs. Blackwater-Younge said firmly, seating herself in the chair opposite Arabella. "I thought red, green, and white stripes, since we are coming into the Christmas holiday season, and perhaps white flowers." She smoothed out her gloves in her lap and smiled at her sister-in-law in such a way as to make Arabella feel a momentary pang of guilt about her plans to attend a very disreputable function. "It is really too bad of Beast to go out of town like this, but then again, one doesn't really need him about when one is planning a ball. My dear Rondo is never of the least use in these cases. It is all 'Just as you wish, my love,' and 'Whatever would suit you best,' with *men*," she added darkly. "Thank heaven I shall be rid of this dreadful mourning by then. Did you know they read the will, and Rondo's aunt only left us that great awful Jacobean parlour set she kept in the front room in Bath? To think that I had to go into black gloves for that dowdy stuff—well, we'll just give it to Sally and Arthur, they're furnishing a house at Melton Mowbray, and of course when one is hunting, one really doesn't care what the guest rooms look like, does one?"

Both the Russian ambassadress and Beast's sister

looked as if they were settling in for a comfortable afternoon's gossip and planning of the ball; from her reticule, the princess had withdrawn a set of notes on the guest list and the caterers, and Mrs. Blackwater-Younge was most anxious to discuss the news from Italy concerning Princess Caroline's most recent transgression, so no more could be said about the projected expedition to Vauxhall Gardens, much to Arabella's annoyance and Alexi's obvious relief.

Both ladies were firmly determined to do their duty by their protégée, and determined equally that her first ball given as Lady Blackwater should be a resounding success. To this end, with the long experience of two veritable doyennes of polite society, they were ruthless in their culling of the guest list and absolute in their dictums concerning the proper caterer (Gunter's), which wines should come up from the cellars laid down by Beast's Italophile grandfather (claret, Madeira, hock, and sherry) and which should come from Gunter's (champagne), the menu of the dinner for twenty given before the ball (seven courses and seventeen removes), the two bands to be engaged for the evening (the Pandean Pipes during dinner and the Household Dragoons' Orchestra for the ball proper—so much better with the waltz), the number of card tables to be set up in the green salon (five, as well as the billiard table in the billiard room for anyone who cared to play, and gentlemen could smoke there and in the library), and the style and type of refreshment to be served during the ball (lobster patties, cheese tarts, cold ham, two epergnes of fruit). Beast would have to raid the forcing houses at Blackwater and send up whatever he could find, and perhaps a pineapple or two could be found somewhere in London, if a ship had come in from the West Indies. That, and an assortment of pastries and other sweet delicacies from the kitchens, should suffice even the heartiest appetite.

"After all," Princess Lieven said darkly, "one only has to recall Mrs. Hyde-Parker."

"She was socially ruined, you know, when she gave a ball and only served a dozen lobster patties," Charlotte kindly explained to Arabella. "That was in your mother's time, dear, you would not remember, but everyone else does."

Arabella could only nod, open-mouthed, and the two ladies plunged onward into a tour of the cold and drafty ballroom, with its wall sconces of human hands in gilt bronze and its Linnel chairs stacked in the corner.

"I daresay one could fit a hundred or so dancers into this space," Princess Lieven judged, shuddering slightly at the human-hand wall sconces.

"We had four hundred at my come-out, and it was a dreadful squeeze," Charlotte remarked off-handedly, smiling as she looked about herself, perhaps recalling the days of her youth when she lived in this house. "Several ladies fainted, but that may have been as much from the effect of tight lacing as the crowd, you know. And one of them was Sally Allbright—she always was one to call attention to herself, anyway. Oh, the times we had then, the gentlemen all in brocades and the ladies all in grey powder—these days just do not seem the same to me, somehow," she said, sighing.

"Whenever I think of the fashions of the *Directoire*, I have to close my eyes," Princess Lieven remarked, pulling back a curtain to peer out into the garden. "Nothing more than scraps of muslin, and nothing to keep you warm but a shawl—especially in Russia, now *that* was terrible—it is a wonder one did not die of pneumonia."

"I really think, dear, that you could remove that portrait of Barbara before the ball," Charlotte said in an aside to Arabella before she and the princess took their leave, full of macaroons and Madeira, and thoroughly satisfied that they had done their duty to their protégée.

"I don't think that my husband would like it," Arabella said doubtfully.

"Believe me, he will never even notice," Charlotte replied wisely. "Besides, it is you who are mistress here now, *not* Barbara—and for that we are all grateful!"

Again, Arabella felt a pang of guilt as she kissed her sister-in-law's cheek, but it was not enough to keep her from pinching Count Baransky's arm as he sought to make his departure. She whispered, "Nine tonight—come for me in a hackney and we'll go from there to the theatre."

He rolled his eyes, but Arabella was not to be moved. Placing his high-crowned beaver on his blond curls, he shook his head, certain that no good could come out of such a harebrained expedition.

Chapter
Thirteen

"YOU WOULD NOT BELIEVE what trouble I had smuggling these things past Eliza, my maid, you know! I swear she has eyes in the back of her head, which in general is not a very bad thing, but when one has finally decided that one is going to have an *adventure*, it is the last thing one desires!"

As she spoke, Arabella unfolded a silken domino and mask of lavender, which mingled with an aura of camphor and antiquity that permeated the already noisome ambience of the hackney coach.

Count Baransky pressed a handkerchief against his nose. "An *adventure*," he said bitterly. "She calls it an adventure. To judge by the musty smell of that rig, you must have unearthed it from a tomb." His own black domino and mask rested, neatly folded, in his lap.

"Not a *tomb*, precisely, but a trunk I found in the attics," Arabella said, unmoved by her friend's assessment both of their proposed evening out and of her costume. "I think it must have belonged to Beast's mother. These revels used to be quite fashionable, you know."

"I say, Arabella, you couldn't have chosen a more obvious gown. Everyone in London must know that straw-colored dress by now. You might as well leave your card with the maître d'!"

Arabella glanced down at her frock. "It's jonquil satin and Madame Celeste says it's all the crack, and besides, I haven't worn it to death."

"Just don't look to *me* if someone recognises you, that's all," the count said gloomily. "This wasn't my idea, after all." With a sniff he withdrew his elegant Meissen snuffbox from an interior pocket and dipped deeply in the style that had become all the rage among the dandy set.

"Oh, Alexi, please don't be a goose," Arabella pleaded. "My domino will cover my dress, after all, and you could hardly expect us to see anyone who might know us."

"Well, you never can tell," Alexi pronounced thoughtfully. "Should have gone to Lady Jersey's ball tonight. Was dying to sport my blue waistcoat. Daresay it will set a style."

"Yes, I am certain that it will, and therefore you ought to save it for some really important event, not just a rout ball." Noting her friend's Russian gloom, she set herself to the task of raising his spirits with a mixture of supportive remarks and judicious flattery, to which he was by no means impervious.

She did not suceed as well as she hoped, for it was a natural part of Alexi's character to predict dire results for any venture not of his own devising. Happily this effect was balanced by an equal tendency toward a sanguine disposition, and by the time they had arrived at Vauxhall

Gardens, he was well launched into an exposition upon his own talents as a poet, always a happy and distracting subject for his mind. "The opening line should be, of course, 'When Aurora comes, clothed in the shades of dawn,'" he was saying when he broke off. "Arabella, close up your domino! You can see far too much of that dress, you know!"

Arabella did as she was bid, and adjusted her mask for good measure.

"Listen, they are playing one of Spohr's waltzes," Arabella said as the count paid out the two shillings apiece that would admit them past the huge and surly doorman and into the inner sanctums of Vauxhall Pleasure Gardens.

It was a scene that Arabella would not forget. If it was not precisely all that she had dreamed it would be, it was at least very lively, and if her eyes opened very wide at what she saw as the Count lead her into the courtyard, it must be recalled that for all of his reknowned debauchery, Sir Bosworth Ivers, like many other roué, practised a stern morality where his own home and family were concerned.

A red-liveried orchestra played on the bandstand for the curious assemblage below, involved, somewhat raucously, in the dancing of the waltz, although hardly in the staid and respectable manner in which Arabella had always seen it danced in the homes of the great and genteel.

Indeed there was nothing at all genteel about a fête at Vauxhall Pleasure Gardens at the very best of times. With the licence granted persons who are both masked and anonymous, allowed to step from their roles in life for a few hours, the Masked Revels were a saturnalia of no mean degree.

Here all stations and classes of London who could afford the two-shilling admission charge were, for a few hours, democratically equal. Prostitutes, whose clinging dominoes revealed far more of their wares than they concealed, danced suggestively with men whose guises did little to conceal their respectable walks of life. Arabella thought she spotted the gaiters of a clergyman—his arms were wrapped rather well about the opulent form of a very vulgar sort of female whose thin muslin dress did little to conceal a very well-endowed bosom. A respectable-looking girl who might have been a tradesman's daughter was involved with a youth who could have been one of the flash boys from the Seven Dials, to judge by his cocksure manner and coat of a style much favoured by the criminal elements in that neighbourhood.

All classes and all occupations were always represented at Vauxhall, but the Masked Revels had enjoyed for many years a reputation for being particularly debauched, and now Arabella could see with her own eyes that this was all true. A company of burly sailors seated at a table near the dance floor ogled her and raised their tankards in leering salute. Happily she had no understanding of sailor's cant, or else she might have been put to the blush then, if not to instant flight. But Arabella was pluck to the backbone, and she waded into the foray, the writhing mass of bodies, as if she had been an habitué of such scenes. She was only a little relieved when the count bribed a waiter to procure them a free table somewhat out of the central stream of humanity.

In the winter months, the arena was tented over with canvas and illuminated by the light of a thousand candles, but still it was almost stiflingly oppressive with the heat of so many bodies pressed together in so small a place, and Arabella fanned herself, uncertain if her heat was that of embarrassment or environment.

This was the place where apprentices played gentlemen for the night, and whores great ladies. Here the solemn bourgeois let down their guard, and the genteel were as wild as the flash coves who cheerfully picked pockets and boasted about their future fates in Botany Bay or on the gallows.

While the count gave the waiter orders to bring them wine and pastries, Arabella tried not to stare too hard at the activities of the next table, where a very large lady was precariously balanced on the knees of a thin, very thin, gentleman, while her escort looked on in apparent indifference to anything save his wine, of which, seemingly, he had imbibed a great deal. That no one else even gave this vivid tableau a second glance in no way decreased Arabella's feeling that it was somewhat odd, to say the least.

Even if she had wished to communicate her feelings to Count Baransky concerning this event, it would have been quite useless, for the orchestra played at such a volume and the maskers made so much noise that it would have been all but impossible to communicate over the din. And the fireworks, for which Vauxhall was so justifiably known, began in real earnest without, causing a great deal of cheering as well as coming and going of the assembled company in order to have a look at the Catherine Wheel and the name of the establishment in illuminated lettering, as advertised, in several colours and great display.

The orchestra, having completed its rendition of Spohr's waltz, launched into a lively Sir Roger de Coverley, and the sight of so many persons of all stations, sizes, ages and shapes jolting about on the floor provided Arabella with something to think about. So did the bottle of sickly red wine and the plate of equally sickly looking tarts a surly waiter indifferently deposited upon the slightly sticky surface of the table, waiting anxiously for the count to pay him for this remarkable feat, all the while wiping his grubby fingers on a stained apron.

A scantily clad female whose mask did little to conceal

her garishly painted face, and whose thin muslin dress barely concealed her emaciated figure, draped herself about the count's shoulders, whispering enticements into his ear. She completely ignored the presence of his companion, who sipped at the wine and made a face.

"No, no, I thank you," the count said, dumping this vessel of frailty off his lap with no ceremony whatsoever. For this she rewarded him with a torrent of invective so powerful as to make even that sophisticated gentleman nonplussed; she then turned to his neighbour and repeated her initial offer. Here she found willing ears, and a lanky infantryman, his arms about her waist, rose, to the coarse jests of his companions. He disappeared into the nether regions of the place in her company, but not before she had asked for, and after some haggling received, some money in exchange for her favours..

It seemed to Arabella that Count Baransky was indicating, by pantomime, his desire to dance with her. She rose and dutifully followed him onto the floor, where they managed to shuffle about among the large and somewhat noisome crowd in some semblance of movement.

This was marred only by a very large and very drunken Sergeant of Marines taking it into his head that he wanted to dance with Arabella. Much against her own will as well as the count's adamant protests, she was swept away by a pair of rough arms into a rather boisterous romp that fit neither the music nor the crowd. Arabella was bounced and whirled in such a manner as to inadvertently strike a number of other dancers while supported by her oblivious partner.

This person smiled down at her through a mouthful of blackened teeth, but would not or could not listen to her protests. So large was he in comparison to Arabella, who was not a small woman, that she felt, struggle as he might, as if she were no more than a toy in his arms. Unfortunately he was far gone in his intoxication, and would not heed her commands to be set down upon her feet, but continued to whirl her about as if she were of no more substance than a rag doll in the arms of a performing bear.

Some of the other dancers were inclined to take exception to her partner's clumsiness on the floor, and when he inadvertently shuffled backward into an equally burly man who, beneath his mask, bore all the markings of a professional pugilist—broken nose and splattered ears— the boxer simply hauled off and delivered to the sergeant a crushing facer that would have moved Beast, had he been present, to spasms of admiration.

It appeared, however that the Marine was not an admirer of the art of boxing, for with a bearish roar he forgot all about Arabella, dropping her to the floor, and spun in a lurching fashion to confront his attacker.

What followed was a scene that Arabella would never be certain of, but it seemed to her that all hell had indeed broken loose, for suddenly it seemed that the very people who had been happily dancing a moment earlier were now involved in trying to inflict as much damage on one another as possible. Nor were the women much different from the men. The cyprians who, seconds before, had been enticing them with a display of their female charms, had now turned into shrieking harridans anxious to pummel and claw their customers as well as each other, or any other female who stood in their way. The party of sailors by the door, perceiving a member of the armed forces in jeopardy, forgot for the moment their traditional hostility toward the marines and lept into the foray in his defense, brandishing empty wine bottles and cudgels.

Throughout this melee, the orchestra continued to play on as if nothing at all were amiss, while a party of men, obviously employed by the establishment for events

160

such as this, waded, swinging truncheons and bats, into the crowd, perhaps with the idea of restoring peace.

Arabella found her arms being grasped very firmly, and she turned to see Count Baransky, his domino ripped away, his mask askew, leading her with gestures away from the fracas.

She followed him off the dance floor and down a long corridor done up like a papier-mâché grotto, from which a series of curtained partitions extended.

"Are you quite all right?" he asked, pausing to lift a curtain from one of these cubicles.

"I feel a little faint—so silly," Arabella said, gasping.

Never in her life had she fainted, but now, between the excessive heat and the very real fright she had sustained, she felt as if she might. She leaned uncertainly against her friend.

"Pardon me," he said, dropping the curtain and leading her to the next cubicle. "Sure you will feel much better if you just lie down for a moment, Arabella," he said soothingly, leading her into the tiny space in which the single piece of furniture was a sort of a rough couch.

"Th-thank you," she managed to gasp, sinking down on this piece of furniture and putting her head between her knees.

"Lie down, now there's the thing," the count said briskly, removing her mask. "Daresay you were about to faint, Arabella, and that would not do at all. You might have been trampled or worse out there."

Arabella, meekly doing as she was told, stretched out on the couch and closed her eyes. "I am so sorry, Alexi—" she started to say, but he cut her off.

"There will be time for me to say 'I told you so' later, and believe me, it will give me no small amount of pleasure to be able to do so, but for now, I think it is best if you simply lie still, and I will see what I can do about fetching you a glass of water."

Arabella was too weak to protest that she did not want a glass of water, and in fact, did not want the count to leave her in this place alone; the walls were swimming before her eyes, and her heart would not stop pounding wildly.

The count disappeared, and how long Arabella lay still she did not know, but she was a healthy female, and it was not too long before she felt very much more the thing—enough to take a little notice of the barrenness of her surroundings and the interesting noises floating toward her from the other cubicles. Clearly this was a place of casual assignation, and if that explained its popularity, it did very little to reassure Arabella about being there.

She attempted to sit up and rearrange her domino about herself, but it was in sad shreds from the altercation of the dance floor, evidently still in progress to judge by the distant shrieks and shouts and ominous thuds and shattering of glass she heard over the sound of her neighbours. She felt vaguely nauseated, and more than a little light-headed, and it seemed best to try to make herself as still as possible.

Ordinarily a woman of remarkable common sense, as well as of strong constitution, Arabella was a little dismayed by this sudden attack of the vapours, and was mentally taking herself strongly to task for succumbing to such weakness when she heard the curtain being drawn back on its rod and looked up, expecting to see Alexi with a glass of water.

Instead she beheld a tall female in a scarlet mask and domino, accompanied by a strange man, the pair of them staring at her. Too late she snatched up her mask and attempted to disguise herself with it. She would have recognised the hem of that barege dress had she encountered it in the darkness of hell itself; she had no need of the cackle of laughter that identified its owner as none other than Lady Sibley.

"Well, well, well! Do you see what I see?" Lady Sibley asked her masked companion. "If it isn't the virtuous Lady Blackwater herself, waiting, no doubt, for her lover!"

Arabella struggled to find proper words of reply, and could not; her mind was still clouded and her head was swimming.

"I say, Caroline, none of our business," her companion muttered, clearly embarrassed, seeking to draw her away.

But Lady Sibley was not to be drawn away. Beneath the collar of her domino, Arabella caught the glimmer of that detestable diamond necklace, and yearned to scratch it away from that fair neck. "Oh, yes, the virtuous Lady Blackwater, for whom butter would not melt in her mouth, stretched out like a trollop in the grotto at Vauxhall Gardens! I should live to see the sight!"

"Oh, go away, do," Arabella said irritably, feeling as if she were going to lose her supper.

"Oh, I shall, believe me, and by the time I am finished, all of London will know just who I saw! Ha!" Her laugh was drunken, her words were slurred. She was, Arabella realised, far gone in her wine.

"Come away Caroline! Damme!" her companion hissed. "None of our business! Between Beast and his wife, not us! Only suppose we were to be discovered in the same way. My wife—your husband—"

"To hell with your wife, and to hell with that great bobby of a husband of mine!" Lady Sibley's laugh was like a paper cut, and she staggered somewhat on her feet. "It'll all be worth it to see the expression on the face of Beast Blackwater when I tell him about his virtuous lady-wife, the wife he won in a card game with her father—at Vauxhall Gardens!"

"He told you that?" Arabella asked, much distressed.

Lady Sibley threw back her head and laughed. "Of course he told me that. Who did you think he would tell if not his mistress?" she demanded, enjoying this scene as only a cruel and disappointed woman can enjoy the pain of another.

"Sorry, this room is taken," Count Baransky, with the glass of water, had returned. With sick eyes, Arabella watched as he took in the scene.

"Good God!" he exclaimed.

"And if I'm not much mistaken," Lady Sibley exclaimed in high delight, "this must be your lover, none other than the handsome Russian count! Well, you may have everyone else culled, but not me! What a scene! Egad, man, you must have more about you than I thought, to win a woman away from Beast Blackwater!"

She reached out and touched the edge of Baransky's mask, and he drew back as if stung, "I say, madam, I do not know you," he replied in a voice of ice. "Now be good enough to go away."

"Oh, don't you try the cut direct on me, you Russian fop!" Lady Sibley exclaimed. "You know me well enough, as does all of your set! You only choose not to because I'm not good enough ton to suit you! Well, how I shall enjoy the news that Beast Blackwater has called you out and ran you through! To put a pair of horns on him—the likes of you! Ha! What a delicious on dit this shall be, and believe me I shall take the greatest pleasure in spreading it all over London! Perhaps the people who did not believe me when I said that Beast had won his wife from her father in a card game will believe this tale!"

"That is outside of enough, Caroline!" her masked companion exclaimed, forcibly dragging her down the corridor. "I'm taking you home at once! You've had more than enough to drink! Knew I never should have brought you here in the first place, although by God, I swear I'll never take you anywhere again!"

Lady Sibley's voice faded down the corridor in a trail of hideous, mocking laughter.

Arabella and Alexi stared at each other in dismay. She buried her head in her hands and began to sob. "Oh, Alexi, what have I done?" she wailed. "Oh, I am so sorry."

Nervously he soothed her, offering her the glass of water she did not want. "Daresay it's not all that bad! Her credit is no good, you should know that. No one will listen to her. Imagine, spreading stories about you being won in a card game around town! If no one believes that, who will believe this?"

But Arabella refused to be comforted. "Oh, Alexi, I am so sorry," she wailed, then slumped against him. "I am not feeling well. I think I'd better go home."

"I should jolly well think so, after a night like this," Alexi said with great common sense.

Chapter
Fourteen

WHEN ARABELLA AWAKENED IN the morning, she was tucked beneath the crewel-worked counterpane in her own bed with the spindles and the headboard carved with cherubs and roses, in her own rose, green, and white bedroom she had devised herself, in her own house, in Grosvenor Square in London.

As she lay there after a fitful and restless night during which she had only dropped off to sleep at the first light of dawn, she began to wonder if the events of the previous night had merely been some terrible nightmare.

Then she began to feel sickly again, and she remembered with a sinking heart that it had been no nightmare. She had indeed disgraced herself, dragged her best friend into the muck of scandal and allowed her worst enemy the pleasure of triumphing over her.

Without mercy these events paraded before her horrified mind in all their grisly detail, and when the good Eliza came in to draw back the curtains and serve her morning chocolate, she found her mistress being wretchedly sick in the chambermug.

"Lord, my lady, do you suppose it's the influenza?" Eliza asked as she tenderly cleaned up her mistress and helped her change into a clean nightdress before assisting her back into her bed. "They do say there's a bit of it going about."

Arabella, more inclined to put it down to a guilty conscience and a thoroughly bad wine, could only shake her head weakly.

For a moment she considered taking her abigail into her confidence, for there was a great deal of the admirable Fishbank in the maid's character, but wisely she decided the less known, the better it would be for all concerned.

Nonetheless she allowed Eliza to fetch her a hot brick for her feet, and to feed her barleywater and soda bread toast, and to rub her temples with lavender water. This made her feel just a little better, enough to permit Eliza to read several chapters of Miss Webb's latest novel, *Castle Dred,* aloud to her while she lay in bed and tried, without much spirit, to work on her embroidery.

During the course of the morning, there were no visitors, no Mrs. Blackwater-Younge or Princess Lieven arriving to announce that she was socially ruined forever, no Beast thundering up to the door in a towering rage, having somehow had the news in Norfolk and come to murder her and call poor Alexi out—Arabella lived in almost momentary terror, though, of these awful happenings.

Her nausea did subside, however, and for that she was

grateful, in spite of Eliza's remonstrances that Dr. Bailie be sent for; in general her mistress enjoyed such robust health as to cause her the gravest worry when she took a turn as she had done this morning. Eliza finally contented herself with a lecture on the evils of large crowds of people in what she described as "sickness weather." Believing her mistress to have taken sick at Lady Jersey's rout ball and come home early the previous morning, she was prepared to fuss at her and over her all day; Eliza was something of a mother hen.

But around noon, Arabella announced herself well enough to get up and be dressed. It was in her mind that her reputation would be lessened if she were to lay out the whole truth before her husband in a letter to be taken by the second footman down to Blackwater Manor, begging his forgiveness as well as his advice in the matter.

Eliza was a great deal annoyed when she would not accept lunch, a bit of chicken in a light celery sauce and some out-of-season asparagus, prepared by the chef expressly to tempt an invalidish appetite. But Arabella was not hungry; her anxiety was far too great to allow her to eat, and instead she closed herself up in the library, pacing back and forth across the carpet and wringing her hands in alternate bouts of despair that she would be ruined by Lady Sibley's gossip, and hope that the whole matter would be passed over as merely another example of her husband's mistress's sour grapes.

Several times she sat down to the escritoire and seized up the pen in her hand, meaning to set down the basic facts to be sent to Beast, but each attempt met with failure, as once again the ugly situation paraded through her mind like a waking nightmare that would not go away.

She roundly castigated herself for a fool for ever wanting to set foot in Vauxhall Gardens, and again and again mentally flagellated herself with the things she *could* have said, *should* have said to put her despised rival in her proper place. Set-down after blistering set-down rose to her mind, but provided only cold comfort to her troubled mind.

Indeed these images were soon replaced with the picture of Beast receiving the news of his wife's indiscretion (precisely from where, in Norfolk, he would hear this table, she was not entirely certain, but could imagine the lip-smacking satisfaction Lady Sibley must even now be enjoying at penning a few harsh lines, couched in such terms of flattery and deceit that only a man could fail to read between the lines and apprehend the truth). Like the hero in an extremely bad melodrama, Beast would clutch the deadly letter in his fist, his other hand over his wounded heart. He would ride posthaste and in an increasingly foul and murderous temper, toward London, where he would order her out into the street and waste no time in challenging the hapless, gentle Alexi to a duel of such certain fatality that she could easily see the count's bloody and wounded body lying lifeless on the heath, an innocent victim of her own folly and stupidity.

This was enough to send her into a bout of tears, for her mind was already overwrought through excitement and lack of sleep, and her judgement was distorted beyond reason.

No matter what, she was utterly and forlornly certain that Beast would never listen to her protestations of innocence, and that their marriage was as good as over. Oh, perhaps he would not throw her out of the house, but it would be just as well if he did, for she *knew* he would return to Lady Sibley to seek consolation. She had disgraced all of the Blackwaters with her hoydenish conduct. Doubtless good, sweet Charlotte would never speak to her again, and Rondo would look at her so sadly, as if to say he had expected better things from her. Princess Lieven would give her the cut direct, as well Arabella would deserve it, for the trouble into which she had led poor Alexi. From Lady Jersey she would receive a strained little note informing her that she would no longer be welcome at Almack's, so very sorry. But worst of all would be Beast's expression whenever he looked at her—if indeed he would look at her, which she very much doubted. That she could not bear. He was, she thought sadly, the only person she had ever known in her life who had ever been well and truly kind to her, and even if he could never, ever love her as much as she loved him, only see how she had rewarded his kindness.

This was cause for fresh tears.

Arabella was still drying her eyes when the first footman opened the door and announced, in somewhat surprised tones he had not yet learned how to conceal, that there was a visitor belowstairs waiting to see my lady.

Unconsciously Arabella steeled herself, a Mary Stuart on the way to the block, drawing her shawl about her shoulders and pulling herself up to her full height, not forgetting to stuff her handkerchief into her sleeve. "Is it Mrs. Blackwater-Younge or Princess Lieven?" she asked, ready to meet her accusers.

The footman, handsome as footmen are supposed to be, shook his head. "No, my lady. It's Sir Bosworth Ivers."

Arabella gave a nervous little laugh. It was almost a relief to know it was her father.

"Show him up, please," she said, and collapsed back into her chair.

Under ordinary circumstances, she would have wondered what in heaven's name had moved her unfond parent to call upon her after such a long period of time, but these were not ordinary circumstances. When that gentleman arrived, red-faced and puffing from his journey up the stairs, father and daughter merely stared at each another for several moments without either greeting or speech.

Sir Bosworth, if anything, was even more obese than the last time his daughter had seen him, and of a decidedly more florid cast of feature. His immense belly quivered as he heaved himself into a chair and fanned himself with his hat.

"I don't suppose," he said, looking about himself, "that you have anything to drink hereabouts?"

Mechanically, Arabella moved to the cupboard where the sherry decanter was kept and poured him a glass, which she handed to him.

He accepted it greedily, downing the liquid in one swallow. "Better leave that decanter here," he said, wiping his forehead with an enormous handkerchief.

Arabella placed the crystal decanter on the table next to him and sat down in the chair opposite, folding her hands nervously in her lap, twisting *her* jaconet handkerchief out of her sleeve.

"Good Lord, what a set of stairs Blackwater has here! Daresay it will not do my heart any good, all that climbing. You could have received me in one of the salons downstairs, you know." His tone was pettish.

Arabella bit back the retort that rose to her lips.

The sherry seemed to mollify him somewhat. He leaned back into the wing chair with a satisfied grunt, crossing his ankles, his knees separated by the overhang of his belly straining the buttons of its Carleton House waistcoat. He poured, emptied the glass and poured again before he spoke.

"Suppose you know why I am here," he said at last.

Arabella's fingers began to shred her handkerchief into her lap. She dropped her eyes and, in spite of her best efforts, a single tear rolled down her cheek and fell on her bodice.

"I suppose," she said bitterly, "it's all over town!"

"Good God, I should hope not!" Sir Bosworth exclaimed, horrified. "Why, Prinny would never speak to me again if it were! Only fancy! A man in my position must be discreet, you know!"

"Yes, yes, your position! How could I have forgotten *your* position?" Arabella asked ironically. "Of course it must all affect you—or come back to affecting you. How could I have forgotten?"

"Well, it's only a matter of five hundred pounds," Sir Bosworth edged, harrumphing and squirming in his chair. He ran a finger along the inside of his collar. "No more than pin money for you, of course."

Arabella looked up. "Five hundred pounds—I do not precisely understand—oh, of course!" Enlightenment dawned on her, and she wearily shook her head. "You have another gaming debt you cannot pay. Of course, I should have known."

"Yes, yes, that's it. Told Beast I should call on you, you know. Just seems that I never got around to it until today. And it just so happens that last night I dipped rather deep at whist with Prinny—" His eyes took on a crafty look as he continued. "Well, of course I *meant* to call on you before this, of course I did, see how you were getting along and all of that, quite think about you all the time, indeed I do, but it happened out that I was in the neighbourhood, and thought perhaps you might be able to cough up the ready for your papa."

"I see," Arabella whispered.

"Well, dash it, girl, it's only pin money to you, daresay that gown you're wearing cost more than a mere five hundred quid, certainly you can spare it to your own poor papa—I say, Arabella, are you crying? Can't see why you'd be crying, living in a place like this, with servants at your beck and call and—well, I say, Beast don't *beat* you, do he?"

"No!" Arabella cried. "But he *ought* to! I have been so very wicked!"

"Wicked? You? Likely to be Lucy who's wicked, she's developing a tongue on her as sharp as her ma's, but not you! You've always been as good as gold, my little Bella! Come now, it cannot be all that bad!" With awkward and somewhat delayed paternal concern, her father rose unsteadily to his feet and placed his hand on her shoulder.

"I went to Vauxhall Gardens last night and was seen!" she said, sniffling. "By Lady Sibley!"

"Whoa!" Sir Bosworth cried. "Vauxhall Gardens? That's a properly improper place for a young lady to be seen and no mistake. And by Caroline Sibley, too, you say? She did not by any chance, tell you that *I* had told her everything about your—well, your rather sudden marriage, hey?"

Arabella looked up at her father. "*You* told her that?" She sighed, resigned, making a futile gesture with her hands. "What else could I expect?"

Sir Bosworth harrumphed again. "Well, you see, I had a wager with her on the boxing mill, and of course I hadn't a feather to fly with, you know, and so—well, damme, Arabella, it's not as if it wouldn't get out sooner or later anyway. Listen, do you have five hundred pounds? I'd lief as not encounter your husband when the two of you are thatched out this way—"

"Beast is in Norfolk, and I don't know when he'll come back, but I daresay that wretched odious female wasted no time in appraising him of my folly!"

As has been noted, like many another libertine Sir Bosworth was something of a Roman parent when his own offspring were concerned, and he puffed out his cheeks at the idea of his daughter in Vauxhall Gardens. "Daresay he won't like it above half," he said thoughtfully. "Not at all the thing to do, you know. Never would have let you do that when you lived at home!"

"I went with Alexi Baransky, who is a particular *cisceorne* of mine! But of course it looked awful, especially since Beast does not like Alexi."

"What, that dandy from the Russian embassy? You'd choose a man like that over a man like Beast Blackwater? I say, now, Caroline Sibley's one thing—a man can't help himself, you know, not with a woman like her around, but a female, now that's different entirely, especially since you ain't produced an heir yet!" He shook his head sadly. "I expect, if things had been different, your stepmama would have explained this all to you—"

"Much luck to me!" Arabella said bitterly, "If Stepmama should tell me anything! Anyway, Alexi is only a friend and it is all quite innocent, I assure you! How could it be otherwise?"

"By God, Arabella, I do believe you're in love with Beast Blackwater!" Sir Bosworth exclaimed baldly.

Arabella's response to this was to burst into fresh tears.

Indifferent to the tantrums and torrents of his two youngest offspring, perhaps because of their frequent use of such emotion to achieve their ambitions, Sir Bosworth found himself profoundly affected by the bitter, hopeless crying of his eldest daughter, who rarely displayed her emotions. Himself of a suggestible and volatile temper, however shallow it might have been, he felt his own eyes watering in sympathy. "I say, I say, it can't be all that bad! No need to make yourself a watering pot over the affair! Here now, my girl, you've gone and made me cry, too, that won't do, oh, no!"

He blew his own rather large proboscis into a spotted kerchief, patting Arabella on the shoulder in a somewhat ineffective, if highly dramatic, way.

Arabella glanced up at her father. Seeing him dissolved in tears was enough to affright her into a renewed burst herself, and for several minutes neither father nor daughter could speak for weeping.

Perhaps at that moment they were closer in spirit than they had ever been previously in their relationship, for Sir Bosworth composed himself eventually and ventured to say, "Well, I suppose you'd better tell me all about it, my girl!"

And so Arabella did, painting herself, in her misery, as the stupidest female in existence and the most wretched creature on earth, and finishing with, "And to make all of it even worse, I lost my domino and mask!"

It might have been expected that Sir Bosworth Ivers, being very much a man of the world, would have laughed off his daughter's exploits as a childish prank, and pooh-poohed the very idea that anyone with a ha'p'orth of common sense would listen to the jealous and vindictive rantings of a woman who was well known to be Beast Blackwater's former mistress—a female of dubious integrity at the best of times.

But not only was Sir Bosworth singularly lacking in the virtue of common sense himself, he also took a very dim view of any but the most innocuous behaviour in his female dependents. He frowned most dreadfully, puffing his lips and cheeks in and out, and pressed the tips of his fingers together over his vast belly. If Arabella had understood that he was enjoying his belated role of concerned parent to the fullest, and also calculating how best this situation could profit himself, she might have been less attentive to his advice.

But she had no one else to whom she could turn, and indeed, was on the verge of hysterics. So she placed her faith in her father, feeling there was little choice.

"Perhaps, my dear girl, it would be best if you came home," Sir Bosworth pronounced.

Arabella shook her head. "No, that would not do at all! Stepmama and my sisters—"

"Say no more! I am well acquainted with their ways! However, your stepmama has taken the girls off to visit her sister Rosalba in Bath, where there is an entire regiment stationed at the moment! I believe she hopes somewhere in those thousands of men, she might find suitable husbands for Lucy and Harriet, but somehow, I have the feeling I shall have them on my hands for the rest of my life! So you may come home without fear of remonstrance from that quarter—at least until after the holidays!"

Arabella was about to protest, but she could see no other course. To stay at Blackwater House in the wake of the terrible scandal that would surely descend on her head, to face Beast, was more than she could bear. Going back to Half Moon Street was, to her mind, a highly unpleasant solution, but she could see no other.

"You are right, Papa," she said at last with a sigh, rising wearily from her chair. "I shall pack a few things together, and leave a note for Beast, although God only knows he will doubtless rip it into shreds!"

"I don't suppose you would have five hundred pounds laid by anywhere, would you?" Sir Bosworth reminded her hopefully.

"I suppose in the housekeeping money there might be a few hundred pounds laid by for emergencies," Arabella said listlessly.

"Whatever you can find," Sir Bosworth replied. He settled back in his chair, as happy now as he had been in misery only a moment ago, rather like an overlarge baby. From the fruit bowl he selected an apple and bit into it. "I could certainly use whatever you could find. Take your time, take your time. I shall just sit here and enjoy this very lovely house. Such a shame, such a very great shame," he continued lightly as Arabella moved with a slow step out of the room and up the stairs, her heart breaking.

Chapter
Fifteen

"WIFE! WIFE! I AM home!" Beast called as he strode through the door of Blackwater House, his driving coat of sixteen capes covered with dust from the roads, and bearing in his arms a brace of pheasants shot on his estates.

For several moments, only a vast and empty silence returned his greeting. Somehow Beast Blackwater had expected a door to be flung open upstairs and Arabella to appear, wreathed in smiles and floating downward to greet him, dividing her energies between issuing commands to the servants and soliciting assurance on his well-being and the success of his journey.

At first he was mildly irritated when this did not happen, and he assumed that she was out on some pleasure jaunt. And indeed, he might reasonably ask himself, why should she not be, as he had not concerned himself with directing any information to her concerning his return from Norfolk. Beast, not greatly given to any concerns save those of his own interests, did not pause to reflect upon this, but frowned in a most forbidding way at the first footman who appeared to take his coat and hat from him.

"Well, well," he said, "and where is Lady Blackwater today?"

Nervously, the footman accepted the pile of gloves, scarves, cloak and hat laid into his arms, licking his lips before he ventured to offer the reply that all the household had been dreading. "Well, sir, several days ago Sir Bosworth Ivers called upon my lady, and she had Eliza, her maid, you know, pack up some of her things and off she went with him, leaving no instructions save as how the household was to continue to run until you returned, my lord."

The footman cleared his throat nervously, watching his employer with some wariness; Beast, unlike his wife, was known for his tempers.

Beast's heavy eyebrows drew together in a most alarming fashion. "With Sir Bosworth, hey?" he rumbled, stamping the snow off his gleaming driving boots, heedless of the Axminster beneath his feet. "With Sir Bosworth?"

The footman nodded. "She left a note for you, my lord, on your desk in your study. A sealed note," the footman added, as if Beast had accused him of opening it and making the entire household apprised of its contents. Indeed, if Arabella had not sealed it so, the entire household would have known. As it was, they were all agog with curiosity and as much in the dark as Beast himself.

"I see. That will be all, James. Fishbank is downstairs unloading the rest of the goods and game I brought back from Norfolk. You may go and help him. Pay particular attention to the way in which he hangs the game! It is for my lady's ball dinner!"

James bowed, and was surprised to have two pheasants added to his burden as Beast took the steps two at a time, heading for his study.

The drive had been long and cold, and not much aided by a sudden snowfall that had begun to cover the roads and render them into pits of slush and mud.

Beast was tired and somewhat out of sorts from the difficulty of the journey, and put out by the lack of a helpmeet to greet him with a warm fire, a hot meal and a glass of wine. However preoccupied by his own miseries he might have been, he was not so blinded as to not feel a vague prickle of apprehension when the name of his father-in-law had come into the conversation in regards to Arabella's disappearance from Blackwater House, but he naturally assumed some unspeakable family emergency. That such an emergency would either end up costing him a great deal or putting him into mourning at a most inconvenient time were the thoughts foremost in his mind as he strode through the door of his study, a small room just off the library, and picked up the note lying on his desk, sealed with a bit of his own wax.

"Damn and hellfire!" he swore beneath his breath. "Can't she even use her own sealing wax?"

He slid his fingernail beneath the blob and broke the seal, his lean, dark face saturnine as he scanned the closely crabbed lines of Arabella's rather rounded, girlish fist:

Husband,
There will be no need for me to Explain the Necessity for me to absent myself from your life. Rather than bear your reproaches for my *Conduct* I have accepted my father's offer to Shelter my poor head. I hope you will find your Happiness, even if it is in the arms of

Another. Believe me, I shall always wish you Only the Best.

[Here several lines had been crosshatched into oblivion.] I Believe, in Time, you will see that my withdrawal Was the Best Move for both of Us.

I remain, Sir,
"Arabella Ivers-Blackwater"

"Good God!" Beast exclaimed, all at sea. A second perusal of this missive was no more enlightening than the first, and Beast found himself becoming exasperated. "Why cannot women say what they mean and mean what they say, like a man would?" he asked of no one in particular, crushing the letter in his fist. "Cannot a man go on business into the country without coming back to find his wife has run away to—to—"

He smoothed the letter out and looked at it again. "To her father's house! Good God! *What* would drive her back to such a den of Gothics? Just because I went into the country for a fortnight on business? It is Blackwater Manor that pays for the clothes on her back and this bloody great ball she wants to have!"

Lord Blackwater was still fulminating over the vagaries of the female sex when there was a knock on the door and Fishbank entered the room, still in his travelling clothes, a very grave look on his usually jovial countenance. "My lord," he began.

The viscount turned to look at him, a glower on his thin face. But Fishbank had seen far too many of his master's tempers to be intimidated by them, and strode across the floor to procure a glass of sherry from the cabinet for his master.

"It's blue ruin a man needs at a time like this, not fortified lemonade," Beast grumbled, but he accepted the glass from his man nonetheless, downing its contents before glowering at Fishbank and asking, "Well, what do you know of this?"

Fishbank, noting the level of sherry in the decanter had dropped noticeably since his lordship's departure for Norfolk, raised eyebrow as he refilled Beast's glass. "From what I have been able to ascertain in the kitchen sir, four days ago, her ladyship's father, Sir Bosworth Iv—"

"I know who her ladyship's father is, may he be blasted to hell's north gate where it never stops freezing!" Beast growled in interruption. "The thing of it is, what the *devil* the old fish said or did that her ladyship should go off with him?"

Fishbank shook his head. Clearly he was a little shaken by this unexpected turn of events. He was fond of Lady Blackwater, whom he had found to be a good and reasonable mistress, as much devoted to her husband's interests as was his lordship's servant himself. "As I was saying, sir," he continued a little reproachfully, "Sir Bosworth Ivers was noted to have called upon her ladyship last Wednesday in the early afternoon. It was James who let him in, sir, and he remarked upon the event as being somewhat singular, her ladyship's people not having much been in evidence since your marriage."

"Continue!" Beast commanded, pouring a third glass of sherry down his throat, a dangerous, wolfish glitter in his eyes.

"Begging your lordship's pardon, sir, that is what I was attempting to do!" Fishbank said. "Sir Bosworth and her ladyship were closeted together for perhaps a half hour, according to James, when suddenly her ladyship came out of the library in a great pet, and started to order her things packed up to be taken to Half Moon Street, where Sir Bosworth has his house. And that was all I could get from him. Eliza, her maid, is waiting for you outside. I

181

thought you might prefer to interview her yourself, my lord."

"Send her in!" Beast shouted. "Good God, man!"

Fishbank opened the door of the study and beckoned into the library. Miss Eliza, looking very frightened indeed, did not at first respond to the summons, but merely stared, tongue-tied, at Fishbank. Clearly she was very upset, for she wrung her hands and seemed near tears. At the sight of Lord Blackwater's stormy countenance, she shrank backward a step or two, but Fishbank, made of sterner stuff, took her by the arm and brought her into the study.

"Eliza's my cousin, my lord, and a more honest girl I don't know. Now tell his lordship what you know, girl, and don't be afraid, his bark is far worse than his bite, I assure you."

"Come, girl," Beast said, with an effort to put some kindness in his voice. "What do you know about this affair?"

Eliza pulled up her work apron with both hands and wrung it between her fingers, biting her lips, clearly terrified by the master.

"Her ladyship has been that kind to me," she started, a little defiantly. "You could fry me on a griddle, you could, and not a word would pass my lips that would hurt her!"

Some intrinsic kindness beneath Blackwater's temper asserted itself; he was touched by her loyalty to her mistress. "Come, now, Eliza, is it?" he said in softer tones. "I have no wish to do harm to your mistress, you must know *that*! I only wish to know what provoked her to move to her father's house. Is she ill?"

Eliza raised her downcast eyes and met his lordship's gaze. Something she saw in the depths of those dark eyes must have reassured her, for she stopped fidgeting and ceased to shake like a leaf. Drawing a deep breath, she bit her lower lip. "Well, I don't know about that. The morning she left here, she was right sickish into the chambermug, and she lay abed all morning, which is not like my lady at all. She's one to have her chocolate and be up, for she greatly minds not being at breakfast with yourself, sir." She frowned in recollection. "And it seemed to me that the night before, she was in a rare taking. She and that Russian nobleman, the handsome one, sir, had gone to a rout ball at one of my lady's great friends—"

"Baransky?"

Eliza nodded. "That would be him. The handsome one with the la-de-da manner." She made a broadly feminine gesture with her hand. "Count Baransky, yes, sir."

"I might have known," Beast muttered beneath his breath. "And what then?" he asked aloud.

"Well, she wore her jonquil silk, the one with the white ribbons and roses in lozenges all over the hem and the Peau-de-soie trim on the sleeves, and when she came home, she came home early and just threw it down on the floor, which is not at all like my lady, her being so nice in the care she takes of her clothes, and didn't even wait for me, just crawled into her nightdress and went to bed. I think—" Eliza bit her lower lip. "I think, sir," she said finally, evidently having made some interior decision, "that she was crying, which is not at all like my lady either, her being in general as even-tempered a lady as you could ask for, and not like some I've worked for, always up in the boughs or down in the depths."

Beast pressed his thumb and forefinger into the sides of the bridge of his nose. "Now tell me, Eliza, what happened when Sir Bosworth came?"

Eliza, clearly warming to her theme, continued with a degree of unsightly relish. "Well, sir, like I said, in the morning she was sick, and she lay abed, and then when she did get up, she come down to the library, but instead of playing at her pianoforte as she usually does when there's no socializing to be done, she paced up and down, up and down. At least that's what she was doing when I put my head in to see if she was feeling well enough to be out of bed. She seemed greatly disturbed, iffen you was to ask me."

"And then Sir Bosworth called. Did she send for him, do you know?"

Eliza shook her head, all innocent eyes. "Oh, no sir, because if she had, I would have known, wouldn't I? Or one of the footmen would have taken the message, and no one ran a message for her that morning. Indeed, sir, she seemed right shaken to see him, her father not being, as you might say, a regular visitor in the house. Indeed, that was the first look I had at him, when she come upstairs with him to get him his five hundred pounds from the housekeeping money she lays by in the jewel safe in her room—and to have me pack her things up. Very particular about that, she was, sir. Only was going to take what she needed, she said, and I was to pack the rest of her things up and put them into the attic aside of the *first* Lady Blackwater's. I can't believe it, all those lovely gowns and bonnets, and all she'd take with her was enough to fill a little trunk, just a few plain sort of things and a band-box—".

"You mean she put all her clothes aside?" Beast demanded.

"That's what I'm telling you, sir. Just took a few round gowns and a couple of nightdresses with her. She was proper put out she was, and right distracted. I says to her, I says, 'My lady, what will you do without me?' And she says, 'You stay where you are and take care of things like I told you, Eliza, and you may have that green-and-white striped pelisse you always liked so much, and the chip-straw bonnet to match.' And I says, I says, sir—"

"Her things!" Without a word, Beast tore from the

room, his long legs mounting the stairs toward his wife's bedchamber, Fishbank and Eliza following him doubtfully.

Beast threw open the door of his wife's bedroom. The rose-and-pink counterpane was spread neatly across the big carved bed, and the curtains were sensibly drawn lest the thin winter sunlight fade the Aubusson rugs. Everything sat neatly and sensibly in its place; the fainting couch was where it had always been, its striped cushions plumped and neatly arranged. The conversation set by the cold fireplace was not even out of order by an inch. Everything was as neat as it could be, but, he noticed with a sinking heart, all traces of Arabella's presence had been removed. No half-read novel lay opened on its spine on the nightstand, no single slipper, casually removed and forgotten, rested beneath a chair. Not even the ivory comb and brush set that had been her mother's lay in its place on the pier table by the window.

With a mounting sense of panic that transcended a mere burst of ill temper, Beast flung open the doors of the rococo wardrobe, only to find it empty and smelling faintly of rose petals.

The same was true of her dressing room. It was as if she had never tenanted this place, had never been there at all. He pulled open drawers, threw open closets and cupboards and found only emptiness and the faint scent of rose petals she had used to sachet her clothes.

"It's all gone, sir," Eliza said unsteadily from the door. "I packed it up just like she told me to do, and had the footmen stow it away in the attics. Did I do the wrong thing? I only did what she told me. And what about my character, sir? I can't just go away without a proper reference . . ."

The face Beast turned to her was no longer bestial. Instead those long, dark features were full of an agonized, questioning pain, as if he had been wounded and could not comprehend by whose offices, or the reason for the hurt.

"Don't worry, Eliza," Fishbank said quietly, putting a hand on his cousin's shoulder. "You did the right thing, and whatever happens, I know his lordship will not turn you out. Now be a good girl and go attend to some sewing or something. I know you will not let the family down by idle gossip with the other servants!"

"I—I'm sorry, sir!" Eliza blurted out, and picking up her skirt, turned and ran.

Still, Beast stood stock still in the middle of the room. His gaze met that of his faithful servant, and he shook his head, uncomprehending, unbelieving. All thought of rank and station was gone between Beast and Fishbank; they had been together for so long, and through so many different adventures, that there was no need for any sort of verbal communication.

Gently Fishbank touched his master's arm, and like a small boy Beast allowed the younger man to lead him down the stairs and into the warm sanctuary of the library.

Here Beast sat down heavily in his favourite chair, and watched with unseeing eyes as Fishbank lit the fire, poured him another glass of sherry, and prepared the portable writing desk, leaving it at his elbow.

"I daresay a note to Lady Blackwater at her father's will very soon clear up any misunderstanding, sir. Please ring for me when you have completed it, and I will deliver it to Half Moon Street myself."

"An excellent idea, of course," Beast said with a great deal more heartiness. He dipped the pen and scribbled several lines, folding the paper over and handing it to Fishbank.

The good servant touched his temple and smiled. "I shall return very soon," he promised, and departed, as he had done a thousand times before, upon his master's business.

The clock was striking four when he returned to find his master pacing the study. Never before had he seen Beast Blackwater appear so helpless, not even when the crisis with Lady Barbara had reached its peak.

Beast had cast off his coat and opened his neckcloth; otherwise he was still in his travelling dress, and his eyes had a wild and haunted look as he turned them upon Fishbank, still shaking the snow from his shoulders and hair. Just so, he glanced over Fishbank's shoulder as if he expected to see Arabella trailing in his wake. His expression when he did not see her was bitter disappointment.

"Well?" he said in a strained voice. "What happened, man?"

Fishbank drew off his gloves and rubbed his frozen hands together before he replied. "I delivered the note as you requested, sir. It was taken by Mr. Butterworth or Butterbank or whatever, Sir Bosworth's butler, who informed me the ladies had gone to Bath to visit an aunt, and that Sir Bosworth was at his club. I left it with him, and requested that it be given to my lady as soon as possible."

"Bath? Arabella went to Bath?" Beast demanded. "What would send her to Bath, especially with that stepmother of hers and those sisters?"

Fishbank, frozen and exhausted, had put in a long day. That morning he had risen at five thirty to supervise the journey from Norfolk to town, and he had ridden in an open vehicle in the snow and inclement weather all the way, only to turn around again and journey halfway across London in order to be treated with cold incivility by what he would not have scrupled to call a senile old gawby of a butler, who like as not had grown old in the service of that ramshackle establishment on Half Moon Street. Old, and what was more, senile, for not only was the man deaf as a post, he had come down like ugly when Fishbank had attempted, as one man to another, to solicit some news of Lady Blackwater's welfare from her father's chief minion. While he could not say that he had been sent away with a flea in his ear, precisely, he would and could say that old Buttercup or Butterworth or Butterbank had certainly been less than forthcoming when it came to the lady he called Miss Arabella, as if she'd never been my Lady Blackwater at all. Perhaps Fishbank would have shared these sentiments, or some professionally edited version thereof, had he not been thoroughly tired of what he was beginning to feel was a mere turn-up between master and mistress such as had not been known before, but might easily be known again. If my lady had taken a snit in my lord's extended absence and gone off to Bath, what of it?

But then again, he had not read the fatal note.

Wearily, for he too, had put in a rough day, Beast waved his man away. "Thank you, my good Leporello!" he said with one of his rare, charming smiles. "You have done what you can. Now, I suppose, all we can do is wait to see what will happen. Go and have your dinner. I know that you will not gossip about this!"

Fishbank sniffed, offended at the very thought, and took himself off to the world belowstairs, there to quell the runaway rumours with the lofty pronouncement, however inaccurate, that my lady had gone to Bath, called away by the sudden illness of an aunt of her stepmother's.

This did very little to satisfy the curiosity of anyone, even the pot-boy, who was notoriously slow-witted. But such was Fishbank's dominion over the lower regions of Blackwater House that not even Eliza, bursting with what she knew and thought she knew, dared to contradict the stern and repressive look she received from her cousin.

Abovestairs, Beast read and reread the note, no more able to make any sense of it than had it been written in

Iroquois. He did not call for his supper that night, but ordered up another bottle, and then another. Somehow, he could not feel that Arabella had taken off for Bath. Several times he felt a great rush of annoyance that she should be creating such a great stir, when all he wanted was for her to be there, where he wanted her, and to be attentive to his needs, just as he had imagined her so many times during his stay in Norfolk. If it was at all possible, he could have said that he missed her, even within that fortnight's separation, and indeed, had missed her so much that he had cut his visit short by forty-eight hours in order to rejoin her. Had she been at a tea, or a rout ball, or a drum, he might have forgiven her that; after all, sooner or later she would return, and would listen to his adventures in the country and play the pianoforte to soothe his weariness.

He had laboured long and hard in Norfolk upon a hundred projects long neglected, and now he believed that his beloved estates had begun to be set into the order they demanded and deserved. And all the while he had been riding his acres with the good Whitten, or visiting with his tenants, or walking over the acres of the home farm, or gunning the chases, he had thought of Arabella and the pleasure he would have in showing her this other world, this place that to him represented what England was all about in its true essence. Everything he had viewed was seen afresh through her, as if he were viewing it with her eyes, and he had realised, before the first week was out, how very much he had come to depend upon her as a part of his life. While it had never precisely been his intention to inform her of the style and manner in which his feelings had grown and matured toward her, he had returned to London with the resolution that he would treat her with more interest than hithertofore. Beyond that he was incapable, he thought, of expressing his feelings. He only knew that all during the long journey on the London Road, he had anticipated seeing her again, and he had been disappointed.

Again he opened the note, spreading it on his knee and perusing it as if it were a cypher from some ancient and forgotten culture, and again he could discover in it no particular reason for her departure. Couched as it was in the terms of a Cheltenham tragedy, it did not seem at all like her. Her conduct? Another? Into Bath?

In fact, he decided, it sounded rather as if she were leaving him, now that he pieced together the odd phrases.

"Written like a Tragedy Jill," he mused aloud.

He began to feel somewhat put upon. While Beast's understanding was good, like many another extremely masculine man he had some trouble apprehending the vagaries of the female mind, and it was not long before he began to feel *very* put upon indeed.

What right did she possibly have to jaunt off like that, leaving him all alone? Hadn't he always treated her right, given her everything she wanted? Well, it seemed to him, after he'd finished off the bottle of sherry and cracked the brandy, that he was damned ill-used. His pride was fierce, and in his cups, it began to assert itself.

Her conduct, she said.

Baransky?

He had to laugh aloud at that. The very idea of Arabella indulging in a liaison with that fribble of fashion was enough to make him laugh. Alexander Baransky was far more interested in the way his tailor turned his lapels than pursuing a romance, wasn't he?

Well, if that was the way she felt, then let her stay on Half Moon Street! Like a wounded bear, Beast growled into his brandy. Let her stay on Half Moon Street, he thought. It had been a bad idea from the start. No woman would ever treat Beast Blackwater badly again.

Never again!

Moodily he reached again for the brandy bottle on the table beside him, and as he did so, something pricked at his arm.

Cursing, he shifted the cushion beneath his elbow, and withdrew, from the upholstery of the chair, a piece of Arabella's half-finished embroidery.

Slowly he brought it out into the light. It was the needle, still threaded with a bit of green thread, that had pricked him.

With great rough fingers he spread the canvas open, looking at the half-completed pattern of flowers and leaves. She had meant to recover some chairs with this, he recalled vaguely, studying the tiny, intricate stitches.

On sudden impulse, he pressed the canvas against his face, inhaling the faint rose scent of Arabella's sachet.

"Dear God," he said, sighing with a great and terrible sadness. "She has left me."

Chapter
Sixteen

"HAS MISS ARABELLA COME out of her room yet?"

Sir Bosworth, allowing Butterworth to remove his great-coat, glanced up the stairs as if half expecting to see his eldest daughter emerge from her chambers at that very moment.

The elderly butler shook his head. "No, although I took a tray up to her this evening. Lord Blackwater's man came by. Apparently his lordship is back in town. He left a note for Miss Arabella, which I placed on the silver tray here on the hall table—indeed, sir, it is gone now! Miss Arabella must have come down when my back was turned and fetched it upstairs."

Both men looked at the empty tray sitting in its accustomed place on the table in the vestibule.

"A bad business, a very bad business!" Sir Bosworth said, sighing gustily. "How was I to know that m'wife and the girls would take it into their heads to return from Bath so soon?"

"You may be certain that I told his lordship's man nothing at all!" Butterworth said. "One hates, Sir Bosworth, to see Miss Arabella so plagued."

"Quite right, quite right," Sir Bosworth said, and had almost reached the sanctuary of his study when he was pounced upon by Lady Ivers.

"I might remind you, sir, that the hour is advancing midnight, and you said you would be home by eleven!" she shrieked, and immediately launched into a tirade concerning her domestic woes, with a pair of daughters to launch into society who did not seem to take among the military gentlemen of Bath, and the burden of having her unwanted and ungrateful stepdaughter thrust back into the bosom of the family, and Sir Bosworth's general uselessness as a husband and provider. "The very least she could have done was have a ball for the girls, give them some push into the exalted circles in which she was moving! But no, I thank you! Home she comes because marriage don't suit her!" Disparaging Arabella had long been one of her favourite topics, and it was one she warmed to in shrill and bitter accents, following her spouse down the hall.

From her vantage point behind a cracked door, Harriet Ivers watched her parents pass.

"They're gone," she whispered, turning to her sister Lucy. "Give it to me! I want to see!"

The dining room was unheated, but at this hour of the evening it provided them with a secret refuge from the rest of the household.

As Lucy leered unpleasantly and turned away from her sister, it could be seen that she was clutching a piece of paper to her scrawny bosom. "No!" she hissed. "Me first!"

"I was the one who snatched it up when Butterworth wasn't looking! I want to see it first!" Harriet cried.

Lucy rounded and delivered her sister a smart slap.

"Owww!" Harriet whined. "You are the greatest beast in nature, Lucy! Me first! Me first! I'll tell! I'll tell Mama, and then you'll see!"

"Oh, be quiet, do! You'll have them all down on us, and then Papa will read us a huge lecture about reading other people's letters, and that would be a dead bore!"

"Well, I want to see what she did! After all, it's only Arabella. Butter wouldn't melt in her mouth and she comes home and locks herself in her room and won't even let us try on her fine clothes! Pah! Pah to her! Let's see!"

The two girls bent over the contested piece of paper and Lucy broke the seal.

"It's from her husband!" she hissed.

"Let me see!" Harriet attempted to snatch it out of Lucy's hands but she resisted, and with a little dry sound the letter ripped into several pieces.

"Now you've done it!" Lucy hissed, "See what you've done! Now there will be the devil to pay!"

But the resourceful Harriet was on her knees, gathering up the fragments. Her lip trembled and it appeared as if she would go into one of her notorious crying fits, but Lucy made a gesture as if to slap her, and she quieted down.

"What can we do? If Papa sees this, we will be in trouble!"

"It was your idea," Lucy said. "I'm going to tell."

"Just you try and do that," Harriet replied. "I'll tell about how you met Mr. Moberley behind the churchyard and kissed him!"

"Look!" From the mantelpiece, Lucy took down the tinderbox. "We'll burn it, see, and no one will ever know."

Neatly, or as neatly as they could, the girls piled up the sad fragments of Beast's letter and ignited them.

"Don't you tell," Lucy hissed, pinching Harriet very hard. "If you tell, I'll kill you, and I mean it this time."

Oblivious to the little dramas happening below, Arabella sat by the window in her small and unheated room, wrapped in her shawl, staring out the window at the grey and snowy rooftops of London.

Chapter
Seventeen

PERHAPS IN CONSEQUENCE OF the unusual circumstances surrounding his marriage, since he had married Arabella Beast had practised the most temperate of habits, having only the occasional glass of wine or beer, at most a bottle of champagne when celebration was demanded, instead of the four or five bottles of wine or brandy generally consumed by one gentleman in a sitting.

But now, alone and feeling deserted and at a loss to explain why Arabella should flee his house to return to that hellish ménage on Half Moon Street, he lapsed back into the habits of his bachelor days.

How much time had passed since he had closeted himself in the library with its ample store of brandy bottles, he did not know. Outside the grey light of a snowy London day had slowly darkened into night.

Although the lamplighter had come and made his rounds, illuminating Grosvenor Square with the new gaslighting, Beast made no move to so much as strike a candle within the shadowy room where he sat motionless, save to pour out another glass.

Once, Fishbank had attempted to knock on the door to demand of his master whether he wanted dinner in the dining room or sent up on a tray. He received with equanimity the curses and insults hurled at him through the closed and locked mahogany doors, and went away to impassively inform the staff that his lordship was not to be disturbed for any reason.

Since the household was in turmoil following her ladyship's sudden departure from Blackwater House, this announcement was met with the feeling that it was something of an understatement, but even so, the house-maids, fearing Beast's legendarily black tempers, tiptoed past the closed door on any errand that might force them to pass that way.

As for Fishbank himself, he settled down impassively on a footman's chair in the hall to await further devel-opments. It spoke volumes for his knowledge of his master that he was in perfect faith of the viscount's ability to be moved to a plain of action, whatever it might be, and that his cooperation would be expected.

Besides, he knew that his master would need him if he happened to drink himself into a stupor, as he had done at the time of the first Lady Blackwater's elopement to Italy.

Thinking about that dark time, Fishbank shuddered and hoped with all his heart that this Lady Blackwater would prove his confidence in her by behaving very differently from the impetuous Miss Barbara.

Unfortunately it was all too simple for a man in Beast's

condition to also recall his first wife's behaviour, and, in his intoxication, to suspect his second wife of imitating rather too well the first. That Arabella had never given him the least cause to suspect her mattered not; in the darkness and the bottle, it was an easy matter to allow the spectre of Barbara to enter into his calculations.

With trembling fingers, Beast smoothed Arabella's note on his knee, and even though the light was too far gone to be able to read her writing, it was as if the words *my conduct* were self-illuminated. *Could it possibly be that while he was away, she had indulged herself in some sort of an affaire with that coxcomb Russian?*

Sober, the idea was ridiculous. Alexander Baransky was hardly Beast's idea of the sort of man who would turn a prosaic woman's head. But then he had also underestimated that damned Pole who had stolen away his Barbara. And, true, Alexi Baransky was just the sort of man a woman would find attractive, if Beast paused to think about it. Blond and blue-eyed, with the face and form of an Adonis—or, at the very least, some idol of the stage or opera. Could Arabella really develop a tendre for a man who crimped in the curls in his hair with an iron? He wondered, incredulous. But then, he only had to remember that Baransky was just the sort of man who was always available to escort a woman to a ball, or to some other form of deadly dull entertainment a man like Beast would have preferred slow torture to attending. Day after day he could be depended upon to haunt a lady's drawing room, advising her on such female fribbles as the colour of her ribbons or what to say to the lady who had attempted to cut her two weeks ago last Tuesday at the theatre. Always a willing ear to listen, a shoulder to cry on, a sympathetic murmur of advice at the proper time. A little gift here and there, a bibelot, a snuffbox, a bouquet of my lady's favourite flowers, out of season. Procuring her favourite bonbons from a confectioners halfway across town. Knowing everyone and everything about the latest on dits and the latest fashions, complete to a shade. Yet seemingly so innocuous, so, well, *effeminate* in those great starched dandyish collars, with his mirror-preening, that even the most suspicious husband would have no qualms in allowing him to dangle about his wife while he went off after the manly pursuits of boxing, racing, sporting events . . . a Don Giovanni in the guise of a Bond Street beau, so outwardly sincere and sympathetic, inwardly planning his seductions with the cold eye and icy heart of—of a woman like Caroline Sibley!

"By God!" Beast cried, so moved by the vision he had conjured up that he rose, however unsteadily, to his feet, knocking over the brandy bottle and the table on which it reposed.

Was that it, then? He wondered, full of fury. Had that man-milliner in the entourage of that Byzantine princess cousin of his seduced Beast's wife with his European charm and his Oriental ways?

Perhaps even now he was planning further snares for Arabella. Perhaps she was not on Half Moon Street, but in Albany Place—or worse, Bath—carrying on an assignation perpetrated by that vile Russian seducer!

Beast had drunk just enough to make him mad with rage, and uninhibited enough to act upon it. With a terrible roar, he threw open the door of the library.

"Fishbank! My hat and my cloak! We're going to Albany Place!"

Nothing that his master could do would ever astound his servant. Wakening from a light dream in which he had envisioned himself as the proprietor of a snug little public house in Norfolk, not far from Blackwater Manor where he was born, Fishbank barely saved himself from a tumble off his chair.

One look at his employer told him it would be futile to remonstrate, and with a sigh he took himself off to fetch his own and his master's cloaks. "Faithful Leporello indeed," he murmured, sighing in a long-suffering fashion to himself. "As if I were some half-witted Italian batman! And when I think how I believed with all my heart that we were finally settled down when my lady came!"

In general, the night porter of the fashionable buildings where Count Baransky took rooms was quite used to the spectacle of intoxicated gentlemen appearing at all hours in search of their resident friends, and he could be persuaded with a coin to allow them access to the apartments.

But there was something beneath the exaggerated, drunken dignity of Beast's manner, some sense of danger, that made him wary of this dark gentleman with the thin face and the animal glitter in his deep-set eyes, and he attempted to curb his passage.

"'Fraid, sir, that the count is indisposed—" he tried to say, blocking Beast's way.

But Beast set him aside as if the burly man were made of a straw, like a Guy Fawkes. "He won't be indisposed to see *me*!" Lord Blackwater thundered, striding up the stairs two at a time.

The porter was about to put his whistle to his lips when Blackwater made a gesture, and with a sigh, Fishbank prevented him from seeking assistance by pinning his arms behind his back, with surprising strength for such a short man.

"So sorry," he said cheerfully, "but my lord does as he pleases. Be a good sort of a fellow and there's a coachwheel in it for you."

The porter knew when he was defeated. "Still and all,

rules of the house!" he said, being the sort of man who needed the last word, which he punctuated by biting into the guinea Fishbank offered as soon as he had released the man.

Blackwater was up the stairs, his long legs carrying him with a surprising swiftness for a man in his cups.

With his fist he pounded on the door of the count's apartments, the sound rumbling in the night stillness.

"Open up, Baransky, I know you're in there!" he thundered. "My God, sirrah, open up, I say!"

In a few moments the door opened a crack, and Alexi Baransky himself appeared, looking more than a little startled.

"Dashed bad ton, Blackwater—" he started to say, but Beast, noticing out of the corner of his eye that several other residents were peering out of their doors at the commotion, put his shoulder against Baransky's portals and pushed his way into the room.

"Where is she?" he demanded in a terrible voice. "By God, sir, I shall call you out to answer to honour!"

The count, somewhat in disarray, his body clothed only in his shirt and an exquisite dressing gown, took a step backward, holding up his hands to deflect a possible blow from the man who towered over him in a thundering rage.

"Please, I beg of you, not in the face, Beast!" he exclaimed. "I should hate to ruin my features!"

This place of vanity only served to enrage Lord Blackwater even further, and he flushed a dark purple, clenching and unclenching his fists.

"Damn your face!" he exclaimed. "Where is she, you man-milliner, you seducer! I know she's here!"

Baransky took a dancing step backward, his eyes as round as saucers, his mouth hanging open, unable, from fear, to form words.

"By God, if I weren't a sporting man, I'd plant you such a facer that your nose would be flattened, sirrah!" Beast roared. "What have you done with her? I demand the truth—and then satisfaction!"

The count, who was anything but a physical gentleman, was quite paralysed with fear, and could only open and close his mouth without forming words. His knees shook and his face drained of blood until he was as white as his shirt. Without his shoulder pads and his artfully tailored breeches, he was a very small and somewhat puny man, and when Beast strode forward and in a swooping gesture picked him up off his feet and began to shake him as if he were an annoying lap dog, his eyes rolled back into his head as if he were about to faint.

"*Where is she?*" Through a haze of red, half-crazed rage, Beast could feel himself digging his iron grip into the smaller man's shoulders, their faces only inches apart.

Nothing warned him of the assault that came from behind, and as he felt a sudden weight on his back, and a pair of long-nailed hands raking his face and neck, he bellowed and dropped Count Baransky to the floor, where he lay in a stunned and frightened heap, half swooning.

Open-mouthed, Beast beheld a familiar figure in a scarlet peignoir swoop protectively over the count's recumbent body, glaring up at him with a rage that nearly matched his own.

"You leave him alone!" Caroline Sibley shrieked, cradling Baransky's yellow head in her arms and glaring fiercely at Beast. "You just leave him alone right now! You certainly had your chance with me! There's no need to come storming in here in the middle of the night making a great fool of yourself!"

As if someone had released a valve, the rage drained from Beast's mind and body like water, and he turned as white as he had been previously purple.

"G-Good Lord! You!" he said weakly.

"And who else would it be?" Caroline Sibley asked. She bent over the hansome count. "Oh, my dear, did that terrible man hurt you?" she asked with a completely unexpected tenderness, stroking the count's face.

In response, Baransky could only moan weakly.

"Make yourself useful and bring the vinaigrette from my dressing case in the bechamber," she commanded Beast.

Meekly he did as he was told, not failing to notice all the evidence that he had interrupted a clandestine evening between the two persons least likely to find one another.

His mind was still reeling when the count, resting upon a sofa and somewhat restored by the application of the vinaigrette, a glass of brandy and the surprisingly tender ministrations of Lady Sibley, was able to speak.

"Good Lord, Beast," he said, looking at Blackwater with an accusing eye, "Caroline assured me you two were a thing of the past!"

"As indeed we are!" Lady Sibley put in vehemently. "Really, Beast, I don't see why you had to create such a dust! Now it will be all over town! Not that I much care for that," she added in her old spirit, pulling her peignoir closed over her opulent bosom.

"Mistake. Sorry," Beast said. "I was looking for someone else. I never thought—that is—well, damme!"

"And why should you?" Lady Sibley asked. "You gave me my congé; certainly I have the right to seek happiness elsewhere!"

Looking at the pair of them, it struck Beast that they were more than simply attracted to each other, that somewhat deeper feelings—or as deep as two rather shallow people could enjoy—were involved, and in spite of himself, he almost laughed aloud, so incongruous was the scene.

"Daresay you might wonder about us," Count Baransky said, always concerned with the opinion of the world in his affairs. "Came about in the oddest fashion. After that dustup Arabella and I had with Caroline in the Vauxhall Revel—"

"You and Arabella—" Beast began, then wisely and discreetly stopped himself.

"Yes, daresay she must have told you all about it," Baransky continued naively. "Well, it was my fault, you know, I shouldn't have taken her, no matter how hard she pleaded with me, but she can be devilish set on her mind when she takes an idea into her head, and after that brawl, when I took her into the grotto to lie down, her head was swimming so, and Caroline happened to see us in what must have looked like damned odd circumstances—well, daresay you know, and you know that is not what is between Arabella and I at all!"

"I was a trifle foxed and I acted very badly. Can you forgive me, my darling?" Caroline Sibley cooed, holding the count's hand against her bosom and gazing at him fondly.

He smiled in a moonstruck manner. "Of course, my love. I could forgive *you* anything." They might have lapsed into a fit of billing and cooing had not Beast cleared his throat to remind them of his presence.

"Well, the thing of it was, Arabella was dead certain Caroline would spread the story all over town, and of course it would put you in a rare taking, and you must know that she loves you beyond anything—"

Beast made a noise, but restrained himself. "Pray continue!" he asked.

"Well, since it was partially my fault, you know, for taking Arabella to Vauxhall in the first place, and I was not anxious to have *you* against me, let alone that sort of gossip going about Arabella, I went to call on Caroline the next day, and—well, so you see it!"

"It was like a bolt from the blue," Lady Sibley said fondly. "Right in my drawing room."

"So Caroline won't tell a soul, and the fellow she was with certainly will keep it to himself, for if his wife found out—well, anyway, there you have it." He took Lady Sibley's hand into his own and gazed into her eyes in a rather syrupy fashion, Beast thought.

For a moment Lord Blackwater sat absolutely still as the pieces fell together in his somewhat disordered mind, and he began to ascertain the truth of the situation.

Suddenly he threw his head back and began to laugh, a sound as rich as it was rare. "The little goose!" he exclaimed. "And that father of hers no doubt saw a way in which he would turn it to his own profit!"

The happy couple stared at him, benevolent as happy lovers were wont to be with the world, but also faintly puzzled.

Beast rose. "Thank you! This has been most enlightening! Most enlightening indeed! I hope you will forgive me for disturbing you at such a moment, but please, I hope you will accept my best wishes for your future happiness and no hard feelings!"

The count murmured what was polite, but Lady Sibley only gave him a sideways look. He knew that it was not in her character to forgive nor to forget, but he also understood that the Blackwaters were no longer the targets of her deep and treacherous talents for spite.

"Quick, Fishbank!" he cried as he came running down the stairs, flinging his cloak about his shoulders before braving the snow. "We must find a hackney for Half Moon Street!"

Chapter Eighteen

SINCE HER RETURN TO Half Moon Street, Arabella had not slept well, and when she did sleep, her dreams continued the great unhappiness she felt in her waking hours. The news she had received that afternoon did not, as it should have, add to her peace, and as she tossed fretfully on her bed, her mind returned again and again to this new problem until she was reduced to a state of exhaustion that imitated sleep.

The scratching at her windowpane did not at first awaken her, but as it continued she unwillingly rose into consciousness and opened one eye, expecting to see the cook's cat demanding admittance after a nocturnal prowl.

When she beheld the shape of a human face staring through the frosted pane at her, she sat bolt upright and clutched the sheets to her chest, certain she was having yet another bad dream.

"Arabella!" called a muffled yet familiar voice, and the face suddenly dropped out of sight.

Feeling as if she had finally gone mad, and at the same time wildly hopeful, Arabella sprang out of bed and padded across the icy floorboards in her bare feet, throwing up the sash.

"Husband," she heard her voice coming out with a surprising mildness that wildly contradicted the torrent of emotions she was experiencing, "*What* are you doing?"

"Right now, I am hanging my fingers from your windowsill and it's a damned long drop to the kitchen roof!" Beast managed to say, looking up at her with a wild grin, clearly enjoying this. "Let me in, Arabella, I need to talk to you."

"You're foxed!" she exclaimed, apprehending Fishbank, who stood on the kitchen roof below his master, obviously rendering what aid he could in this project. He bowed, and, distracted, Arabella waved to him as if it were the most normal thing in the world.

"I was foxed—terribly foxed, but I'm not now! I'm cold dead sober, Arabella, now be a good wife and let me in!"

She grasped his wrists and pulled, and he braced his boots against the side of the house, and together they managed to draw him in through the narrow window.

"Lord, it's colder in here than it is outside!" he said, blowing on his hands and dusting the snow from his hair and shoulders.

"My stepmother does not believe in fires in anyone's room but her own," Arabella said drily, lighting a stub of a candle and pulling on her robe and slippers. "Be quiet, do! Only wake up the household and there will be *such* a turn-up!"

"Let them all wake now or sleep 'til Judgement Day, it's all the same to me!" Beast exclaimed.

Arabella looked at him strangely. She had never seen him in such a mood of happy wildness, and intuitively she understood he was enjoying this adventure. And so, she recognised, was she.

Somehow this seemed highly improper, and recalling herself, Arabella was about to remonstrate with him when Beast seized her firmly in his arms and lifted her chin with his thumb and forefinger so that her gaze met his darkly sparkling eyes.

"Now," he said sternly, "you are a great goose, and I am a sound fool, but before you enact me a Cheltenham tragedy about how you've created a great scandal with Caroline Sibley and Vauxhall Gardens and that silly fribble Baransky, none of which should plague you in the least, much less drive you away from me—well, I am going to tell you something I have been too proud and too blind and too selfish to say to you before!" He took a deep breath and continued onward in a rush. "I love you, Arabella! You are good and kind, and gentle, and I know now that if I should lose you through my own folly, I would lose the greatest happiness I have ever had in my life! There, I have said it aloud, and you know that such words don't come easy to me!"

Arabella could only stare at him with wide eyes, nonplussed.

"What's more, you don't have to love me—I know I'm not a sort of lovable fellow—I'm selfish, and I've the devil's own temper, and well, I'm aware that I haven't given you a great deal of the sort of things that females like, great fancy compliments, dancing attendance on your every move, escorting you to all the ton parties, that sort of thing, but if that's what you want, I'll do it, well, some-times! More than I do now! I'll even go to Almack's with you—I'll try to become the—the cavalier servant you must dream of! Even though I'm damned awkward at that sort of thing," he added a little dubiously.

"Oh, no, please—" Arabella whispered. "Husband, I—" She tried to turn her head away, but Beast held her fast.

"No, you must hear me out!" he declared, his great brows drawing together, his thin lips searching to form the words coming from his soul. It was a struggle; this was not at all what he was accustomed to, and finally he stopped his struggle, shaking his head and smiling ironically. "Beast Blackwater, who fears nothing, afraid of speaking his heart to his own wife! Arabella, I would as soon face down a grizzly bear with a stickpin as try to—try to, well, there you have it! See how I shake?" He placed his long, thin hands on either of her cold cheeks, so that she had to look at him, and Arabella noted that his hands were trembling. She placed her own over them, shaking her head from side to side.

"Beast, you hurt me so much when you say these things about yourself! It is I who have been stupid and senseless and jealous and conniving, and you have been only good and kind and generous with me, and—and better than anyone I know! I love you!"

"Well, why didn't you say so a long time ago?" he asked. "It would have saved us both a great deal of trouble, you know! Because, well, damn, Arabella, *I love you!*"

"I was waiting for you to say that first," Arabella pointed out, not unreasonably. She smiled. "If you don't mind, please will you say it again?"

Beast swallowed hard and screwed up his courage. "I—love—you," he tried, then let out a loud whoop of laughter, lifting Arabella off the floor in his arms. "*I love you!*" he cried joyfully. "*I LOVE YOU, ARABELLA!*"

"That is nice, my love, but not so loud—"

"Let the whole world know! Shout it from the dome of St. Paul's! I love you, I love you, I love you! Three small words, and so damned hard to say and now I am saying it!" He spun her about, more than pleased with himself and with her.

Arabella was quite breathless, but she did manage to interject, "And I love you, more than anything in this world, Beast, save there is only one thing—"

He looked extremely doubtful, and lowered her to the floor again although he kept her in his grasp. "One thing?" he repeated cautiously.

Arabella frowned and bit her lower lip. "Husband, would you *very* much mind not seeing Lady Sibley any more?"

Beast looked blank. It took him several seconds to even recall precisely who Lady Sibley was; of late his thoughts had centered exclusively upon Arabella. "Who? Oh, her," he said dismissively, bringing Arabella's most unhappy suspicions to a close in two words. "You didn't think—oh, my poor little wife! Why did you not say something before? *That* has been over since the day we were married! You thought that I continued that liaison— oh, my poor Arabella!"

"You mean you and she are not—"

He shook his head, smiling at her.

"Oh, dear," Arabella said with a sigh. "What a little idiot have I been, eating myself out with jealousy—"

"And I thought you and Baransky—"

"Alexi! What, Alexi?" Arabella opened her eyes wide in surprise. "Alexi is far more interested in his cravats and his dreadful poetry than me!"

They looked at each other.

"Why didn't you tell me?" they both asked at once.

Very gently, Beast embraced his wife. She surrendered herself to the circle of his arms and sighed happily.

"You see," she said, a little out of breath, "I knew I was falling in love with you and I was so afraid that if you found out, it would give you a disgust of me—after all, ours was a marriage of convenience and you said—"

"Blast what I said! I was a man properly blue deviled that day—half out of my mind with the aftereffects of drink—I thought that *you* preferred it that way . . . and that you would be hurt and repulsed if I were to . . ."

Arabella shook her head. Her smile put to rest all his fears on that point, and slowly he brought his mouth down to hers in a way that she found most pleasant.

"Now," she said when he had released her after several highly pleasurable moments, resting her head against his chest, "I feel truly married."

Before Beast could reply, the door creaked open on its hinges and they both turned at once to the sight of Sir Bosworth Ivers in his dressing gown and slippers, his nightshirt slightly askew, clutching, like a weapon, a brass candlestick in one large fist. He blinked once or twice at the sight that met his eyes, and relaxed his demeanour slightly.

"Oh, it's you, Blackwater! Very well, then! M'wife is certain we've been invaded by housebreakers and will all be killed in our beds!" He shook his head at female folly. "It would seem that you and Arabella have made up your differences, then."

Beast grinned, but did not relax his clasp about Arabella's waist. "Yes, sir! And if you have no objections, I should like to take my wife back to her own house this very dawn!"

Sir Bosworth, never at his best in the mornings, merely shrugged his agreement. "Just as you like! Shouldn't stay here myself if I didn't live here!" He nodded politely and turned to go, then, never being a man, no matter how drowsy, to miss a main chance, he turned back again into the room. "I say, Blackwater, while you're here, I don't suppose you'd care to lend your old pa-in-law a few hundred quid till quarter-day?"

"Papa!" Arabella exclaimed in warning tones.

Sir Bosworth shrugged. "Well, no harm in asking, is there?" he said, sighing, and turned again, shaking his head, to make his exit. "Men on the kitchen roof, she says, murderers and housebreakers, as if this were the Ratcliff Road—"

Beast and Arabella looked at each other. "Fishbank!" they both said at once and went to retrieve their servant before he was taken up by the watch.

"Now," Beast said, opening the window and accepting the assistance of his wife, "Why do I feel, for some odd reason, as if from here on in our lives will be that of a Darby and Joan, a Beatrice and a Benedict, and that the rest of our times will be dull compared to this moment. Here I am, a great block of a husband, half hanging out a window, a half-frozen servant on the roof below in terror of being taken up by the watch, a father-in-law who will, upon every meeting, seek to borrow a few hundred pounds till a quarter-day that shall doubtless never come, and a wife who is such a very great fool that she loves, yes loves—an arrogant wretch like me?"

Arabella's lips brushed her beloved's cheek. "I suppose it is just because you are a most fortunate man," she replied with a little chuckle. "From now on, I intend to keep you firmly beneath the cat's paw, following you from room to room, demanding to know your most secret thoughts and feelings."

"And you shall be forced to listen to them in great and excruciating detail, I promise you," Beast said, returning her kiss with gusto.

"Do you know," he said after a moment, "I daresay Fishbank could be sent home—but we have waited long enough!"